Praise for Atiq Rahimi

A Curse on Dostoevsky:

"Atiq Rahimi brilliantly reimagines *Crime and Punishment* and, in a daring feat of creative panache, transplants Dostoevsky's classic morality tale to modern-day Afghanistan. This is easily Rahimi's most imaginative and complex work yet, and should cement his reputation as a writer of great and unique vision."

—Khaled Hosseini, author of *The Kite Runner* and *A Thousand Splendid Suns*

"This book . . . breathes the very dust of Kabul, the geography, both personal and political, of its alleys and districts. Welcome to Kabul, [a place] with faith but without laws."

—*Livres Hebdo*

"This is more a novel to chew over than gobble down."

—Anthony Cummins, *Sunday Telegraph*

"Here, Atiq Rahimi sings an incandescent, raging story, which dissects, in a highly sensitive way, the chaos of his homeland and the contradictions of his people." —*L'Express*

"'If we all decided, today, on the example of this young man, to put our own activities on trial, we could conquer the fratricidal chaos that is currently reigning in our country.' This is the function of remorse even in a land in turmoil. It is not a luxury. *A Curse on Dostoevsky* is a gift to literature."

—*Le Figaro*

"In the light of the Russian writer, [Rahimi] describes his country so that we may understand it like we never have before. His latest novel isn't only breathless, beautiful, and strong, it is indispensable . . . He dared—and succeeded."

—*Le Point*

"Most certainly his most ambitious work yet."

—*Libre Belgique*

"Wide and bewitching, rich in numerous psychological and metaphysical devices . . . Atiq Rahimi may have achieved his best work in the French language."   —*La Croix*

The Patience Stone:

"[*The Patience Stone*] is a deceptively simple book, written in a spare, poetic style. But it is a rich read, part allegory, part a tale of retribution, part an exploration of honor, love, sex, marriage, war. It is without doubt an important and courageous book."

—From the introduction by Khaled Hosseini, author of *The Kite Runner* and *A Thousand Splendid Suns*

"*The Patience Stone* is perfectly written: spare, close to the bone, sometimes bloody, with a constant echo, like a single mistake that repeats itself over and over and over."

—*Los Angeles Times*

"Powerful . . . an expansive work of literature."

—*New York Post*

"In this remarkable book Atiq Rahimi explores ways through which personal and political oppression can be resisted through acts of self-revelation. He reveals to us the violence we are capable of imposing upon ourselves and others in our personal as well as political and social relations. In his stark and compact style, Rahimi recreates for us the texture of such violence, its almost intimate brutality as well as its fragility. Although the story happens within the context of a particular time and place, the emotions it evokes and relationships it creates have universal implications and could happen to any of us under similar conditions. *The Patience Stone* is relevant to us exactly because, as Rahimi says, it takes place 'Somewhere in Afghanistan or elsewhere.'"

—Azar Nafisi, author of *Reading Lolita in Tehran* and *Things I've Been Silent About*

"With a veiled face and stolen words, a woman keeps silent about her forbidden pain in an Afghanistan marred by men's foolishness. But when she rediscovers her voice, she overcomes the chaos. Atiq Rahimi tells the story of this woman's heart-breaking lamentation to awaken our consciences."

—Yasmina Khadra, author of *The Swallows of Kabul*

"[A] clever novel . . . readers get a glimpse of daily life in a country terrorized by conflict and religious fundamentalism. Rahimi paints this picture with nuance and subtlety . . . [His] sparse prose complements his simple yet powerful storytelling prowess. This unique story is both enthralling and disturbing."

—*San Francisco Chronicle*

"Rahimi's lyric prose is simple and poetic, and McLean's translation is superb. With an introduction by Khaled Hosseini, this Prix Goncourt–winning book should have a profound impact on the literature of Afghanistan for its brave portrayal of, among other things, an Afghan woman as a sexual being."

—*Library Journal*

"A slender, devastating exploration of one woman's tormented inner life, which won the 2008 Prix Goncourt . . . The novel, asserts [Khaled] Hosseini in his glowing introduction, finally gives a complex, nuanced, and savage voice to the grievances of millions."

—*Words Without Borders*

A Thousand Rooms of Dream and Fear:

"The language has the rhythm of a Sufi prayer; the novel offers an insight into the deepest fears of the people of Afghanistan."   —*Los Angeles Times*

"That sense of losing one's identity, of being subsumed by a greater, if illogical, power, is a key theme in Atiq Rahimi's taut, layered novel . . . *A Thousand Rooms of Dream and Fear* is the intimate narrative . . . of an entire desperate, anguished country."   —*Washington Post*

"An intensely intimate portrait of a man (and by extension his country) questioning reality and the limits of the possible . . . full of elegant evocations . . . *A Thousand Rooms of Dream and Fear* resonates deeply because, no doubt, Rahimi has written a true and sad account, but the story could easily be that of any other Afghan, of any other denizen of this modern, anarchic state. In the end, we are left to wonder whether Rahimi has presented us with a story, a dream, or a nightmare, though it is likely all three."
                    —*Words Without Borders*

"Rahimi's tale of confused nationality, indiscriminate punishment, desperate survival, and no clear way to safety depicts decades-old events, but it feels especially poignant amid the U.S.-led war in Afghanistan that's spanned the greater part of the past decade."   —*Flavorwire*

"An original and utterly personal account of the pressures a totalitarian society exerts on the individual in 1979 Afghanistan, before the Soviet invasion . . . A flawless translation does justice to Rahimi's taut, highly calibrated prose."
                    —*Publishers Weekly*

"In prose that is spare and incisive, poetic and searing, prize-winning Afghani author Rahimi, who fled his native land in 1984, captures the distress of his people."

—*Booklist*, starred review

"Rahimi is an author known for his unflinching examination of his home country as much as the experimental styles in which he writes . . . *A Thousand Rooms of Dream and Fear* takes risks in its structure . . . But Rahimi's carefully controlled new novel exploits these uncertainties, joining the past to the present and legend with fact, creating an appropriately surreal narrative, one that rings through with truth."

—*ForeWord Magazine*

"A taut and brilliant burst of anguished prose . . . both a wonderful and a dreadful little book."   —*The Guardian*

"A beautiful piece of writing."

—Ruth Pavey, *The Independent*

"Short but powerful . . . The beauty of the language lends this work a haunting clarity."   —*The Herald*

"The novella is verbal photography . . . [it] seems the real thing . . . seamlessly translated."

—Russell Celyn Jones, *London Times*

Earth and Ashes:

"Anyone seeking to understand why Afghanistan is difficult and what decades of violence have done to its people should read Atiq Rahimi. He is a superb guide to a hard and complex land."   —Ryan Crocker, former U.S. ambassador
to Pakistan, Iraq, and Afghanistan

A CURSE ON DOSTOEVSKY

A Curse on Dostoevsky

Atiq Rahimi

Translated from the French by
Polly McLean

Other Press
New York

Copyright © P.O.L éditeur 2011
First published in France as *Maudit soit Dostoïevski* in 2011

Translation copyright © Polly McLean 2013
First published in Great Britain by Chatto & Windus, London,
in 2013

Production Editor: Yvonne E. Cárdenas
Typeset in Sabon LT Std by Palimpsest Book Production Limited,
Falkirk, Stirlingshire

10 9 8 7 6 5 4 3 2 1

Library of Congress Cataloging-in-Publication Data

Rahimi, Atiq.
[Maudit soit Dostoïevski. English]
A curse on Dostoevsky / Atiq Rahimi ; translated from the
French by Polly McLean.
pages cm
ISBN 978-1-59051-547-1 (pbk. : alk. paper) — ISBN 978-1-
59051-548-8 (e-book) 1. Afghanistan—Fiction.
2. Psychological fiction. I. McLean, Polly. II. Title.
PQ3979.3.R34M3813 2014
891'.563—dc23
2013042495

Oh to have committed the sin of Adam!

HAFIZ AZISH, *Poétique de la terre*

But life, like writing, is nothing more than the repetition of a sentence stolen from another.

FRÉDÉRIC BOYER, *Techniques de l'amour*

THE MOMENT Rassoul lifts the ax to bring it down on the old woman's head, the thought of *Crime and Punishment* flashes into his mind. It strikes him to the very core. His arms shake; his legs tremble. And the ax slips from his hands. It splits open the old woman's head, and sinks into her skull. She collapses without a sound on the red and black rug. Her apple-blossom-patterned headscarf floats in the air, before landing on her large, flabby body. She convulses. Another breath; perhaps two. Her staring eyes fix on Rassoul standing in the middle of the room, not breathing, whiter than a corpse. His *patou* falls from his bony shoulders. His terrified gaze is lost in the pool of blood, blood that streams from the old woman's skull, merges with the red of the rug, obscuring its black pattern, then trickles toward the woman's fleshy hand, which still grips a wad of notes. The money will be bloodstained.

Move, Rassoul, move!

Total inertia.

Rassoul?

What's the matter with him? What is he thinking about?

Crime and Punishment. That's right—Raskolnikov, and what became of him.

But didn't he think of that before, when he was planning the crime?

Apparently not.

Or perhaps that story, buried deep within, incited him to the murder.

Or perhaps . . .

Or perhaps . . . what? Is this really the time to ruminate? Now that he's killed the old woman, he must take her money and jewels, and run.

Run!

He doesn't move. Just stands there. Rooted to the spot, like a tree. A dead tree, planted in the flagstones of the house. Still staring at the trickle of blood that has almost reached the woman's hand. Forget the money! Leave this house, right now, before the woman's sister arrives!

Sister? This woman doesn't have a sister. She has a daughter.

Who cares? What difference if it's a sister or a daughter? Right now Rassoul will be forced to kill anyone who enters the house.

The blood veers off just before it reaches the woman's hand. It flows toward a worn, darned part of the rug and pools not far from a small wooden box over-flowing with chains, necklaces, gold bracelets, watches . . .

2

What's the point of all these details? Just take the box and the money!

He crouches. His fingers move hesitantly toward the woman's hand, to grab the cash. Her grip is hard and firm, as if she were still alive and keeping a tight hold on the wad of notes. He pulls. In vain. He looks anxiously at the woman's lifeless eyes and sees his face reflected in them. The bulging eyes remind him that a victim's last sight of her assassin remains fixed in her pupils. He is flooded with fear. He steps back. His reflection in the old woman's eyes slowly disappears behind her eyelids.

"Nana Alia?" calls a woman's voice. It's happening, she's here, the one who wasn't meant to come. You're done for now, Rassoul!

"Nana Alia?" Who is it? Her daughter. No, it isn't a young voice. Never mind. No one must enter this room. "Nana Alia!" The voice approaches, "Nana Alia?", climbs the stairs.

Leave, Rassoul!

He takes off like a wisp of straw, flying to the window, opening it and leaping onto the roof of the house next door, abandoning his *patou,* the money, the jewels, the ax . . . all of it.

Reaching the edge of the roof, he hesitates to jump down into the lane. But an alarming cry from Nana Alia's room makes everything shake—his legs, the roof, the mountains—so he jumps, and lands hard. A sharp pain shoots through his ankle. It doesn't matter. He

3

must stand. The lane is empty. He has to get out of here.

He runs.

Runs not knowing where he's going.

He only stops at a dead end, beside a pile of rubbish, the stink burning his nostrils. But he is no longer aware of anything. Or doesn't care. He stays. Standing, leaning against a wall. He can still hear the woman's piercing cry; he doesn't know whether she is actually screaming or he is being haunted by her cry. He holds his breath. All at once the lane, or his mind, empties of the sound. He pushes himself off the wall to move on, but the pain in his ankle stops him dead. He grimaces in pain, leans back against the wall, squats down to massage his foot. But something inside him starts rising. Suddenly nauseous, he bends over to vomit yellowish liquid. The filthy dead end spins around him. He puts his head in his hands and sinks to the ground, back to the wall.

He is still for a long moment, eyes closed, not breathing, as if listening for a cry or a moan from Nana Alia's house. Nothing but the beating of his own blood in his temples.

Perhaps the woman fainted when she saw the corpse.

He hopes not.

Who was that woman, the blasted creature who messed it all up?

Was it really her or . . . Dostoevsky?

Dostoevsky, yes, it was him! He floored me, destroyed me with his *Crime and Punishment.* Stopped me from following in the steps of his hero, Raskolnikov: killing a second woman, this one innocent; taking the money and the jewels that would remind me of my crime; becoming prey to my remorse, sinking into an abyss of guilt, ending up sentenced to hard labor . . .

And? At least that would be better than running off like an idiot, a pathetic excuse for a murderer. Blood on my hands, but nothing in my pockets.

What madness!

A curse on Dostoevsky!

His febrile hands close around his face, lose themselves in his frizzy hair, then clasp together again behind his sweat-soaked neck. He is seized by a terrible thought: What if the woman wasn't Nana Alia's daughter? She might take everything and leave as quietly as she came. But what about me? My mother, my sister Donia, my fiancée Sophia—what will become of them? I committed this murder for them. That woman has no right to the loot. I have to go back there. Screw my ankle!

He stands up.

Goes back the way he came.

R ETURN TO the scene of the crime? What a trap! Everyone knows it's a fatal error. An error that has ruined many a competent criminal. Haven't you heard that wise old saying: *Money is like water: once it flows away, it never comes back*? It's all over. Never forget that a thief only has one chance at a job; if you mess it up, you're fucked; any attempt to sort things out is bound to end in disaster.

He stops, glancing around. Everything is calm and quiet.

He rubs his ankle and sets off again. Unconvinced by the wise old saying. He walks fast, decisively, until he comes to a fork in the road. There he stops for a moment, just to catch his breath before taking the street leading to the scene of the crime.

Let's hope the woman really did faint next to the old lady's corpse.

Here he is, in the victim's street. He slows down, surprised by the silence around the house. A dog is dozing in the shade of a wall. It sees him and stands up heavily to emit a lazy growl. Rassoul freezes. Wavers.

Lets a little time pass in the reluctant hope that it will convince him of the folly of his curiosity. He's about to leave when he hears footsteps hurrying through Nana Alia's courtyard. Panicking, he flattens himself against the wall. A woman shrouded in a sky-blue chador exits the house and rushes away, leaving the gate open behind her. Is this the same woman? It must be. She has taken the money and the jewels, and is making her escape.

That's too much! Where do you think you're going, you infidel? You've no right to that money, or those jewels. They belong to Rassoul. Stop right there!

The woman speeds up and disappears down a lane. Rassoul ignores the pain in his ankle to rush after her. He catches up with her by an unlit entrance to a building, where he is suddenly stopped in his tracks by running footsteps and the cries of teenagers. Again, he tries to hide by flattening himself against the wall. Despite her haste, the woman also stands aside to let them pass. Rassoul's eyes meet hers through the gauze of her chador as he bends to rub his sore ankle. Then she is off again, in the teenagers' wake, even more hurried and distressed than before.

Rassoul resumes his pursuit, limping and out of breath. At a crossroads the woman takes a new, wider, busier street. Rassoul stops dead, horrified by the dozens of women in blue chadors walking briskly along the road. Which one to follow?

He pushes desperately through the mass of veiled faces, searching for the slightest clue—a bloodstained

hem, a box hidden under one arm, a suspicious haste—
but there is nothing. He feels suddenly dizzy, and has
to make an effort not to pass out. Once again, he is
terribly nauseous. Sweating, he moves into the shade of
a wall and doubles up to vomit more yellowish bile.

Feet pass in front of his dazed eyes. He is exhausted,
becoming less and less aware of the surrounding noise.
Everything goes quiet: the coming and going of the
people, their talk, the cries of the street hawkers, the
beeping of the cars, the traffic . . .

The woman has disappeared. Lost among all the
others, faceless.

But how could she have run off, leaving Nana Alia—
surely one of her relatives—in such a state? All she did
was scream. She didn't even call for help. How cunningly
she must have assessed the situation, made a decision,
and gone off with the loot. Without even committing
murder. The bitch!

Without committing murder, perhaps, but she is a
traitor. She has betrayed her own family. Betrayal is
worse than murder.

This isn't the moment to work up a theory, Rassoul.
Look, someone is trying to give you money, fifty
afghanis.

Who does he think I am?

A beggar. Squatting wretchedly on the pavement in
your dirty, ragged clothes, unshaven, with your sunken
eyes and filthy hair, you look more like a beggar than a
murderer. A beggar who won't even take what's given.

The man can't believe it. He insists, shaking the note in front of Rassoul's distraught eyes. Nothing. So he shoves the note into Rassoul's bony fist and walks away. Rassoul looks down at the money.

The booty from your murder!

A bitter smile plays on his bloodless lips. He closes his fist and is about to stand when a terrifying blast of noise glues him to the spot.

A rocket explodes.

The earth shakes.

People throw themselves to the ground; others run around screaming.

A second rocket, closer and more terrifying. Rassoul joins those on the ground. All around him is chaos and noise. A great fire is giving off black smoke that spreads through this entire central Kabul neighborhood at the foot of the Asmai mountain.

Some minutes later a few heads, looking like dusty mushrooms, begin to poke up in the oppressive silence. Shouts ring out:

"They hit the petrol station!"

"No, it was the Ministry of Education."

"No, the petrol station . . ."

Just to the right of Rassoul, a prostrate old man is desperately searching for something on the ground while grumbling into his beard: "Fuck you and your petrol pump, and your ministry . . . Where are my teeth? Dear God, what's the matter with these marauders of Gog and Magog? My teeth . . ." He rummages around in the earth beneath him. "Have you seen my false teeth?" he asks Rassoul, who is staring at him curiously, wondering if he has lost his mind. "They fell out of my mouth. I've lost them . . ."

"Come on, *baba*, is a set of false teeth really so important in these times of war and starvation?" sniggers a bearded man lying nearby.

"Why ever not?" retorts the old man haughtily, indignant at such a thought.

"What vanity!" snorts the bearded man, standing up and brushing himself off. He walks away with his hands in his pockets, watched suspiciously by the old man, who mutters, "*Kos-madar*, that son of a bitch stole my teeth . . . I'm sure of it." He turns back to Rassoul. "I had five gold teeth in that set. Five!" With a quick glance at the bearded man, he continues in a regretful voice, "My wife was always nagging me to sell them to cover the household costs. I pawned them more than once. Every time my son sent a bit of money from overseas, I would get them back. I only retrieved them from the pawnbroker today at lunchtime. What a shitty day!" He stands up and slips into the crowd, searching for the man, perhaps.

Rassoul appreciated the bearded man's irony, not out of cynicism but because he hates gold false teeth, an external manifestation of greed in all its ugliness. Nana Alia had two herself. If he had had time, he wouldn't have minded pulling them out!

He had had the time, but not the wits; otherwise he

wouldn't be here, wretched, with this fifty-afghani note in his hand.

He stands up among the people who are once again bustling about, running here and there, doing their best to get on with things while covering their mouths and noses so as not to suffocate in the dust and smoke. Most of them are heading toward the blaze. The flames are burning higher and higher. Rassoul approaches too. The burning corpses make him step back, but then a man shouts to him through the smoke for help. He is trying to carry an injured girl on his back. "I'm all alone. This poor young girl is still alive." Rassoul goes to help, takes the girl in his arms and carries her away from the flames before handing her back. "We need to get out of here. The tank is about to explode!" shouts the man, spreading a gust of panic among all those trying to put out the flames.

Rassoul resumes his journey toward the mountain. He stares wearily at the dark, narrow lanes that weave up the slopes, forming a veritable labyrinth, a sprawl of about a thousand houses, all made of earth, built right on top of each other all the way up to the top of the mountain that divides the city of Kabul geographically, politically, and morally, in both its dreams and its nightmares. It looks like a belly about to burst.

From below, he can see the roof of Nana Alia's house. A big house with green walls and white windows.

Now that the woman has left, he can go back, just to have a look around, that's all.

He makes his painful way back up the steep street. He has just reached a building entrance when three armed and raging men burst out of a small side alley. Rassoul bends down to hide his face, so he can only hear their shouts.

"The bastards, now they're blowing up our petrol station . . ."

"Two rockets! Well, we'll hit their station with eight. Their neighborhood will be destroyed, it'll be running with blood!"

They disappear.

Rassoul continues on his way. Before reaching his victim's street he pauses for a moment. His legs are trembling. He is breathing hard. Along with the petrol and explosives, there is a smell of rotting. The air has become even heavier and harder to breathe. There is also another smell: flesh, burnt flesh. Horrific. Rassoul blocks his nose, and takes a step. The second step is hesitant, interrupted by an image of Nana Alia's corpse surging into his disordered mind. There's no way he can go back and look at the corpse he killed with his own hands—these hands that are fluttering, trembling, sweating. Everything must be abandoned. Everything.

He turns on his heel. But a morbid, almost pathological curiosity stops him again. There must be police in the house, relatives, neighbors, tears, wailing . . .

Certain of what he will see, he approaches once more. Even closer. Still nothing. He walks cautiously into the smoky silence of the street, and up to the house. Not a soul. Except that idle dog who no longer even stands up to bark.

Stunned, Rassoul walks up to the front gate. It is shut. He pushes but it won't open. Someone must have locked it from the inside. But then why is everything so quiet, so still?

It doesn't bode well.

Go home, Rassoul!

H E DOESN'T go home. He wanders the city. He's been walking for almost three hours now. Not rushing. Not bothered by his injured ankle, which has already been forgotten. He stops only when he reaches the banks of the Kabul River. The smell of sludge, the fetid stink rising from the riverbed in this late summer, brings him back to himself. As he pauses, the pain returns and stops him from wandering any further. He grabs the guardrail and rubs his ankle.

The air is becoming more and more impossible to breathe. Rassoul coughs. A tickly, noiseless cough.

His throat is dry.

His voice makes no cry.

Not a drop of hope in his mouth, the river, or the sky.

Obscured by a veil of dust and smoke, the old sun goes sadly off to sleep behind the mountains . . . the sun, going to sleep? What an absurd metaphor! The sun never goes to sleep. It travels to the other side of the earth, to shine on happier lands. Take me with you, Rassoul hears himself cry, deep inside. He screws up his eyes, stares at the sun, takes a few steps, and then stops. Shading his eyes with his hand, he looks around anxiously as if to check whether anyone has noticed his silent insanity. Don't worry, dear Rassoul, the world has more important things on its mind than watching a poor madman!

Go back home. And sleep!

Sleep? Is that possible?

Of course. You're going to do just what Raskolnikov did—after murdering the moneylender he went back home and fell into a feverish sleep on his couch. You don't have a couch, I know, but you do have a filthy mattress, waiting compassionately for you on the floor.

And then?

Nothing. You sleep.

No, I faint.

OK then, faint, if you prefer—it doesn't matter, as long as you do it till morning. When you wake up tomorrow, you will realize that this was all a bad dream.

No way, I can't just forget it all like that.

You can. Look, you're not carrying anything to remind you of the murder. No money, no jewels, no ax, no . . .

Blood!

He stops suddenly. Checks his hands in a panic. Nothing. His sleeves: nothing. His jacket: nothing. But then, on the hem of his shirt, a great stain! Why there? No, it isn't Nana Alia's blood. It's the blood of that young girl you saved.

15

The uncertainty disturbs him. He reexamines himself. No other trace of blood. No trace of the murder. How can that be possible?

You probably didn't do it. It was all in your wretched imagination. Your naive identification with a fictional character. Just something stupid like that! Now you can quietly go home. You can even forget that yesterday you promised your fiancée, Sophia, that you'd spend this evening with her. You can't see anyone in this state.

Yes, I won't go. But I'm hungry.

Well, you've got fifty afghanis, so you can buy yourself some bread and fruit. It's been several days since you've eaten.

And so his empty belly draws him to Joy Shir Square. The bakery is closed. An old stallholder is shutting up at the other end of the square. After a moment's hesitation Rassoul starts making his way over to him. He has barely taken three steps when a cry stops him in his tracks. "No, no, don't buy anything!" A veiled woman bursts out of one of the lanes, running and shouting like a maniac. ". . . It's flesh . . . the flesh of . . ." In the middle of the square she stops suddenly, surprised to find it so empty and quiet. She flops to the ground, moaning: "The flesh of young girls . . . the day before yesterday they were handing it out at the mausoleum . . ." Only Rassoul is there, so she spills her tears on him: "I'm not lying, brother, I swear to you. I saw . . . ," she drags herself over, ". . . the offering they gave me," she lowers her voice, ". . . was

16

a young girl's breasts!", she takes her hand out of her chador—"I swear to you, brother . . . it was the same men who were giving out offerings here today . . ."— she pulls off her veil—"the same men . . . the other day . . . outside the mausoleum . . ."; then finally, she is quiet. Wiping her tears with a corner of her chador, she asks weakly, "Brother, do you have any money? I've three children to feed."

Without a word, Rassoul pulls out the fifty-afghani note and hands it to her. She throws herself at his feet. "Thank you, my brother . . . may Allah have mercy on you!"

He walks away, weary of the woman's shouting but proud in his soul.

What a gesture! As if it were that easy to redeem yourself.

No. I am in no way attempting to redeem myself.

So why this act of charity? You're not telling me it was a matter of compassion? No one will believe that. It was simply to convince yourself that you have a good heart, in spite of everything. You may be capable of killing a *loathsome creature* but you can stop a poor family from dying of hunger. Intention is what counts . . .

Yes! That is what counts for me . . .

He stubs his foot on a large stone. The pain in his ankle makes him grimace. He stops, for a moment. Not just walking, but also going over Raskolnikov's words in his head. Praise be to God (or the stone)!

17

It isn't far to the house where he lives. He can walk there, slowly and gently.

When he reaches the gate he pauses for a moment, checking one last time—as well as he can in the fading light of dusk—for any more traces of blood. The same stain remains; a stain that could be either proof of a murder or testament to virtue.

He takes a deep breath before entering the courtyard, which rings with the cries of the landlord's two daughters, swinging on a rope attached to a branch of the single, dead tree. Rassoul creeps over to the other side of the courtyard, to the stairs that lead up to his little room. Just as he reaches the top step, the girls cry out: "Salam, Kaka Rassoul!"

As he opens the door another voice, harsh and threatening, prevents him from going in. "Hey, Rassoul, how long do you think you can keep running off?" It is his landlord, Yarmohamad. Rassoul turns, silently cursing the daughters. Yarmohamad is standing by his window in his prayer cap. "So where's my rent? Huh?"

Annoyed, Rassoul limps painfully back down the stairs, and stands under the window to tell Yarmohamad that he has tried to get his money back, as he promised he would yesterday. But it hasn't worked out—the woman who owed it to him has disappeared. He's been looking for her all day . . .

But he feels a strange emptiness in his throat. No sound comes out. He coughs. A dry, empty cough.

Noiseless, without substance. He takes a deep breath and coughs again. Nothing. He anxiously tries to cry out, a simple cry, anything will do. But still nothing emerges, just a pathetic stifled breath.

What's the matter with me?

"Well?" asks Yarmohamad crossly.

Why won't he just wait! Something serious is happening. Rassoul has lost his voice.

He tries again, taking another deep breath of air, collecting all his strength in his chest to push the words out of his lips. Nothing.

"So did you find this person who owes you money?" asks Yarmohamad sarcastically. "Give me her name, then! You'll have your cash by tomorrow. Come on, give me her name . . ."

If you knew, Yarmohamad, you'd never dare talk to Rassoul like that. He has killed her. And he'll kill you, too, if you upset him. Look at all the blood on him!

Rassoul smoothes down his bloodstained shirt, putting a stop to Yarmohamad's tirade. The landlord withdraws nervously into his room, still grumbling, "What bullshit! Always the same lies . . ." Let him grumble, Rassoul. You know the rest: he'll come back to the window to tell you once more that the only reason he's put up with you for two years is out of respect for your cousin Razmodin; that if it weren't for Razmodin, he'd already have thrown you out; that this is it, he no longer gives a shit about you, or about your cousin, etc.

19

Turn a deaf ear, and go into your room. Don't look around to see if his wife Rona is there.

She is there, of course, behind another window. Watching Rassoul with a sorry expression on her face, as if trying to find an excuse for him. She loves him. Rassoul is suspicious of her. It's not that he doesn't find her attractive. He often thinks of her as he masturbates. It's just that he doesn't yet know exactly what she feels for him—passion, or compassion. If it's compassion then he hates her. And if it's passion, that will cause even more problems in his relationship with Yarmohamad. So what's the point of even thinking about it? Better to go to his room. Better to rest, so he can get his breath back, and his voice.

T HE DRY creaking of the door disturbs a whole army of flies, who had entered in the hope of finding something to eat. There is nothing here. Just scattered books, a filthy mattress, a few shapeless garments hanging from hooks on the wall, and a clay jug in the corner. That's all.

Rassoul picks his way in, kicking aside the books lying around his mattress. He collapses on the bed without taking off his shoes. He needs a moment's respite.

He closes his eyes. Takes slow, gentle, regular breaths.

His tongue is nothing but a piece of old wood.

He stands up.

Drinks.

Lies back down.

His throat is still dry and void, void of sound.

He takes a deep breath, and puffs it out nervously.

Still not the slightest sound.

In a fit of anguish, he sits up and thumps himself on the chest. Nothing. He hits again, harder.

Calm down! There's no need to worry. It's just a throat bug, or some kind of chest infection. That's all.

You need to sleep. If it's still there in the morning, you can go and see a doctor.

He lies down, and turns to face the wall. He curls up—legs bent and hands trapped between his knees—shuts his eyes, and sleeps.

He sleeps until the call to evening prayers, until the gunshots fade on the other side of the mountain. Then there is silence, and it is this disturbing silence that wakes him.

Feverish. No strength to get up. Nor desire, either. Nervous, he tries once more to speak. His breath still comes out strong, but without the slightest sound. More and more distressed, he shuts his eyes again, but the stifled groans of a woman make him jump. He freezes, and holds his jerky breath, listening hard. No more cries, no human noise at all. Intrigued, he labors to his feet, moves toward the window, and glances out past the masses of flies clustered on the pane. In the cold, dull light of the moon the courtyard is sad, empty and still.

After a moment's pause he lights a candle, pulls a small notepad from among the books, opens it, and scribbles: "Today, I killed Nana Alia." Then he chucks it back in the corner, among the books.

He drinks some water.

Blows out the candle.

Lies down on his bed.

On the wall above his worn-out body, the moon casts the shadow of the window frame—a cross.

*It was a spring day. The Red Army had already
left Afghanistan, and the mujahideen hadn't yet
seized power. I had just returned from Leningrad.
The reason I'd gone there is a whole other story,
one I cannot write down in this notebook. Let's
go back to the day I first met you. That is already
almost eighteen months ago. It was at the Kabul
University library, where I worked. You came
asking for a book and went away with my heart.
As soon as I saw you, your modest, evasive gaze
took my breath away and your name filled my
lungs. Sophia. Everything around me came to a
standstill: time, the world . . . so that you and you
alone existed. Without a word I followed you to
class, and even waited for you until it finished. But
there was no way I could approach you, or speak
to you. After that, it was always the same. I did
everything I could to watch you passing, for our
eyes to meet, to smile at you—and no more than
that. Why couldn't I declare my love? I had no
idea. Was it a lack of courage? Pride? Whatever
it was, our entire love affair consisted of that*

fleeting glance and my discreet smile that you may, perhaps, not even have noticed; and if you did, modesty or shyness inhibited your response.

It was this love that brought me to the Dehafghanan neighborhood at the foot of the Asmai mountain, around the corner from you. At the time you lived in a different house, with a beautiful view over the city, right next to those great rocks that I yearned to carve, like Farhad, into your likeness.

Every morning I discreetly accompanied you to university, and then back again in the afternoons. You didn't take the bus—on purpose, perhaps. You walked slowly, your hair covered with a light scarf, your eyes glued to the ground. Your heart was dancing from the fact of being accompanied, even at a distance, by me, your sweetheart—isn't that right? Then, one day, you dared create an incident that would allow me to finally approach you. Not terribly original: you dropped your notebook, hoping I would pick it up and return it to you. But your ruse didn't work! I certainly picked up the notebook, but I never gave it back. I took it with me, gripped tight to my chest like the Koran. And it is in this notebook that I'm writing now.

It was the same notebook he had taken out earlier to scribble: "Today, I killed Nana Alia."

He had also written poems and tales, all addressed

to Sophia, naturally—but which she had never read. For example: "Black is the world. Black is the day. And look at me, Sophia: in this empire of darkness, my heart is leaping. Because tonight, it will be with you!"

You didn't see me. Perhaps you didn't even know that I ate at your house tonight. Yes, I was there, with your father; I even saw your brother Dawoud.

It had been almost a year and two months since I last saw you. More precisely, a year and forty-six days. Yes, that's right. A year and forty-six days ago, I returned to my family in Mazar-e-Sharif. But it no longer felt like home. My father had been so keen for me to study in the USSR, land of his dreams, that he was disappointed when I returned. He couldn't stand the sight of me. After seven months I left them. And when I returned to Kabul, another war had started, fratricidal this time, in which people were fighting not in the name of freedom but to avenge themselves. The entire city had gone to ground. It had forgotten life, friendship, love . . . Yes, that was the city I came back to, looking for you. But you no longer lived in the same house. You had moved, but where to? Nobody knew.

Then today, this afternoon, I went to the chai-khana. It was thick with tobacco smoke, and full to bursting with bearded men. I sat in a corner and drank my tea. My attention was drawn to a

25

man's footsteps as he struggled to make it up the wooden staircase. It was your father, Moharamullah, only now he was missing one leg, and had crutches tucked under his arm. I could hardly believe it. My delight soon dissolved. He was followed by two friends, one with no crutches but limping a great deal and in pain, the other missing an eye and his right arm. All three of them were high, from smoking hash in the basement saqi-khana. *They came over to my corner. I immediately shuffled up to make room for them. Your father sat down next to me. He looked at me sharply, making me smile in spite of myself. The smile annoyed him. In his husky, drawling voice he demanded: "Is it your victory that's making you smile?" and thrust the stump of his amputated leg toward me. "Well, CONGRATULATIONS on that victory,* bradar!*" I swallowed my smile, leaning forward to tell him that I was neither* dabarish, *bearded, nor* tavarish, military . . . *not conquered, still less conquering. Smoothing my beard, I reassured him that it was simply a "gift" of the war. He seemed impressed by this clever response. His gaze softened as he asked me gently where I was from. From here, from Dehafghanan. "This is the first time I've seen you," he said, looking at me carefully.*

I wondered how to tell him that by contrast I knew him very well, that I was in love with his daughter . . .

26

*But I stopped myself. In these times of suspicion
and doubt, it's not right to bother people. So I told
him that I'd just moved to the neighborhood.*

"And what do you do?"

*Just as I was inventing myself a respectable
profession, one of his friends, the one-armed one,
sniggered to the other: "Hey, Osman, look at our
tavarish Moharamullah, he's an investigator now!"*

*"Why did Allah O Al-Alim, the All-Knowing,
create the cat without wings?" asked the lame one,
Osman.*

*"Because otherwise it would have eaten all the
birds in the sky!" replied the one-armed man.
"Praise be to Allah, the Vigilant for not making
Moharamullah a winged mujahideen, or else . . ."*

*They burst into laughter. Your father turned
toward them, annoyed: "Just wait till those winged,
bearded cats arrive and give it to you hard; you
won't be laughing then." This warning just made
his two companions laugh harder. The one-armed
one leaned toward your dad and said: "Chill
out! We're only laughing because we've already
been fucked up the arse!" His reply cracked up
the whole tearoom, including Moharamullah—
everyone except the owner who, conscious of the
talk, said: "Calm down, or they'll be here before
you know it, and they'll ban the* chai-khana *and
the* saqi-khana.*"*

"They will take your chai-khana! *But our*

Islamic bradars *will make sure this country stays full to the brim with hash, saqi-khanas, and fucked arseholes!" replied the one-armed guy, wiping away his tears.*

Everyone laughed even harder. The owner had had enough. He walked over to his counter, grabbed a bowl of water and tipped it over the two cackling cripples. Startled, they stopped. "We've paid to smoke, and now you're spoiling our high!" said the one-armed man, standing up and muttering into his beard. The drenched men left the tearoom.

Your father sat stiffly in his seat. Then he turned toward me, and saw me beaming at him. He couldn't, of course, understand the reason for my happiness. He didn't know that it wasn't his friends' jokes but his presence that pleased me, the fact that I was at last meeting someone from your family; it was a sign from you!

"Don't you laugh at us, young man. It is fate that has made us ridiculous; fate!" He said this slowly, and seriously. After a brief silence, he continued: "Fate . . . we say it is fate that in the end forces the mirror to make do with ashes. Do you know what that means?" He didn't wait for me to reply. "You know that a mirror is simply glass covered with a blend of metals? Well, when time has eroded the metal, the glass is coated in ashes! Yes, it is fate that reduces everything to ashes . . . How old are you?"

"Twenty-seven."

"I'm twice as old as you . . . more even . . . a noble life!" He stared into the middle distance, then continued, "War destroys man's dignity," and stood up. "My heart is bleeding but I have no blood on my hands. My hands are pure . . ." He showed me his palms. "I took part in the jihad myself, in my own way . . ." he moved closer . . . "for a long time I was administrative director of the National Archives. They used to be at Salangwat, just near here . . . It was during the communist era, the first one, the Khalqs. Yes, at the time we had a general director, one of those Pashtun dogs who used to sell all our archives to the Russians. Every time a document disappeared I felt like strangling him. This was the history of our country he was selling. Do you understand? The history of our country! Anything can be done to a population without History, anything! The proof . . ." He didn't explain the proof, letting me find it myself in the ruins of our souls. "In short, there was nothing I could do about that director. He was a Khalq." He spat in disgust and turned toward the owner of the chai-khana, *crying: "Moussa, some tea for this . . . ," jerking his head toward me. He paused a moment, as if trying to remember what he'd been talking about. I reminded him. "Yes, thanks . . . hash . . . wrecks the memory. No, sorry, not hash! . . . Fate . . . fate reduces our memories to ashes! We need*

hash to cope with our fate—a good big dose to blot out all feeling. But how to afford that, these days? If I had any money left, I'd still be downstairs in the saqi-khana.*" I told him that I would pay. He didn't refuse. We stood up and asked the owner to bring our tea down to the smoking room.*

Downstairs, the smoky space was lit by the yellow glow of an oil lamp hung from the ceiling. Men sat in a silent circle around a large chillum, staring into space. They were all high as kites. Your father found us a spot. He smoked, I didn't. Gradually all the others left. When only he and I remained, he continued: "What was I telling you?" And I helped him out again. He went on: "Yes, that dog of a director . . . that dog, whom fate had given wings, was one of these nouveaux-riche types who had heard people talking about whisky, but never tasted it. One day he asked me to get him a bottle. He didn't say whisky, he said 'wetsakay'!" Your father burst out laughing. "Do you know what 'wetsakay' means in Pashto?" Again, he didn't give me time to respond. "It means: Do you want a drink?" He paused, and then turned serious. "I bought him some local alcohol, the worst I could find, and added some Coca-Cola and a bit of tea. It looked just like whisky. I put it in a smart bottle and screwed the top on well. Very professional! I took it to him, and told him it had cost six hundred afghanis. At the time that was a lot

30

of money, you know! And after that he kept asking me for 'wetsakay,' and I kept giving him that same counterfeit alcohol. A few months later his liver exploded. Burst! Finished! Kaput!" He pulled proudly on the chillum and exhaled the smoke up toward the lamp. "So tell me, young man—wasn't that jihad? I too have every claim to being a mujahideen, a bradar, a Ghazi!"

I didn't know what to say. I looked at him sadly. "Ever since that day, I call on Allah and ask him about justice—both his and mine. Listen, young man, that dog of a director was a traitor who needed to be punished. Which is what I did. I couldn't wait for a change of regime in order to take him to court!" Another drag on the chillum, and a pause. "Now the regime has changed . . . These days any idiot thinks he can take the law into his own hands, with no investigation or trial. As I did then. So what! The purpose of punishment is to wipe out the betrayal, not the traitor . . . These days I ask myself whether this kind of law and punishment isn't in itself a crime."

Having been totally absorbed by your father's voice and features I suddenly jumped, and asked him if he had read Crime and Punishment. He looked confused, then burst out laughing. "No, young man, no! Life . . . I have read LIFE!" And suddenly he was quiet. For a long time. I was quiet too. He was smoking, I was thinking. Each of us

31

in our own world. My world was full of you. I was trying to think of a way to get your father to talk about you. Suddenly he began speaking again, but still about his own concerns.

"The era of the Khalq was over; it was the turn of the Russians. Shortly before they left, rockets were raining down left, right, and center. One day the Archives were hit. We were all in the office. Myself and my two colleagues whom you saw just now rushed to save the most important documents from the flames. Then another rocket landed, and all three of us were covered in blood." *He nodded, regretting their courage. "Now, we are disabled. Who gave us a medal? Who remembers us? No one!" Silence, again. Memories, again, and regrets, remorse . . . "Ever since then I stay home with my wife and kids. I have to cover the rent, and feed them all. Who's going to pay for that? When I went to ask for money, they insulted me. They said I was a traitor because I'd worked for the communist regime. So I had no choice; I pawned all those precious documents I had saved. My landlord took them; he knew their value. But then he died. A heart attack. Only his wife and daughter were left, and I had to renegotiate the whole thing with his wife, Nana Alia—and what a bitch she is! A dirty illiterate! Not only did she never give me back the documents, she also increases our rent every month. We no longer*

32

own anything. My poor wife has pawned her dowry items to that cow, and her jewelry . . . And now my daughter has to work for her to pay the rent."

I wanted to stand up and shout, "So that's where Sophia is!" and throw my arms around your father.

"What do you do for work?" he asked, wrenching me from my delight. "What's your name again?"

I told him my name, and that I worked at the university library. After a silence, in which he looked at me tenderly, he said: "I can see that you're an educated man, from a good family." Another pause. "I've two children. A girl and a boy. My daughter is pure and innocent . . ." He stood up. "It's late. I have to go home. She'll be worrying about me . . ."

We left the smoking room and lost ourselves in the gloomy, dusty fog of dusk. After a few steps in silence, your father continued as if he'd never stopped speaking. "But war recognizes neither purity nor innocence. That's what terrifies me. It isn't the blood or the massacres—what frightens me is that dignity and innocence are no longer valued. My daughter, like her mother, is the purest, most noble . . ." Again a silence, a long one this time, that went on until we stopped in front of your house. "This is my house!" he said, opening the gate. Trembling, I moved to shake his hand, but he stopped me. "You're going home? You took

33

me out and walked me all the way here, and now you think I'm going to let you go home?" He invited me in. As soon as I set foot inside I took a huge gulp of air, the air you had breathed. I held it for as long as I could as I followed your father through the little courtyard, under the espaliered vines starting to bud in the spring. I grew more and more nervous, dreading the moment of our meeting. My eyes were darting all over the place, taking in the nooks and crannies of the courtyard, the closed windows of the rooms, and the roof of the house, from which your brother was looking down with a pigeon in his hand. "Hello!" said your father. "Still on the roof?"

"There was a cat wandering around," replied your brother mischievously. Your father turned to me. "That's my son, Dawoud. He's been looking after my pigeons since the schools shut down. I can't get up there anymore." We walked into the house. Your father took me into a dark room and lit a candle; then he left, leaving me to entertain myself by running my foot along the only kilim in the room. I was so excited, my heart racing so fast, that I didn't even know whether to sit down on one of the three mattresses. I wondered if you were aware that I was here, in your house. But no. I wasn't able to see you that evening, my beloved. I left the house after dinner, hoping to return soon.

Another excerpt:

Last Friday, as I was lazing around in bed trying to think of a reason to visit your house, I was rudely shaken from my idleness by the explosion of a bomb that shook the whole neighborhood. Panicking, I rushed out of my room and, finding myself prey to a strange impulse, ran to the site of the explosion. I was transfixed by what I saw. The tearoom was a burning ruin, emanating foul-smelling smoke. Men and women were busy digging bodies out of the rubble. From what they said, I understood that some people had been able to escape but others were still trapped beneath. I started helping them to pull out the bodies. I found your father under a mound of stones, dying. I put him on a wagon and took him home.

And you opened the gate.

Sophia didn't recognize Rassoul with his bushy beard. He didn't introduce himself, either. It was only when he brought round a doctor, and then went off to fetch medicine, that she began to realize she had seen him before. But she was so preoccupied with her father's final moments that she soon forgot the joy of the reunion. That very evening, Sophia's fate lay in his hands, his empty but strong hands.

And so he found a new family who saw him as a

man, a savior, and a protector—important nouns that filled him with pride.

But look at him now, harassed and uncertain, staring into the abyss, lost in dreams, engulfed by nightmares, beneath the moonlight peeking through the walls.

The shadow of the window now shatters over his feverish body.

ANOTHER CRY, the same as before, but louder; then groans, more anguished. They rip through the silence of the room, bursting into Rassoul's sleep. He jolts awake and sits up in bed, holding his breath the better to hear. Where do the cries come from? Who is making them? He does his best to stand, but he is weak. Such pain in his ankle! It's as if his feet are tied. He drags himself over to the window, pulls himself up and peers out at the courtyard. The first thing he sees is Yarmohamad's two daughters standing on the terrace, each holding a storm lamp; they are staring with a strange sort of serenity at the dead tree, just outside Rassoul's field of vision. He heaves himself up a little further. What he sees takes his breath away: Yarmohamad bursting out of the passage with a huge knife in his hand. He rushes over to the naked figure of a woman, her ankles tied by the skipping rope to one of the branches of the tree. Rassoul's horrified gaze swings over to a window, behind which he can make out Rona, also holding a storm lamp. But she is not looking at her husband, or the tree, or her two daughters. She is blowing discreet kisses to Rassoul.

Dazed, he moves a little closer to the window. Yarmohamad spins the woman's body around so that her face appears. It is Sophia. Rassoul screams. A stifled scream, dead in his chest. Yarmohamad starts to slice off the young woman's breasts. Her cries become shrieks. Rassoul, unable to stand, bangs furiously on the window. Unperturbed, Yarmohamad continues butchering Sophia's breasts. Gradually, she stops moaning and crying. Rassoul bashes the window until the pane shatters.

Suddenly, the sound of the door opening, the blinding light of two torches shining in his eyes, and the terrifying shouts of bearded, Kalashnikov-wielding men raiding the room. Rassoul, collapsed amid the shattered glass beneath the window, struggles to get to his feet. One of the intruders rushes over and hits him over the head with his own lamp. The other is rummaging through his piles of books. "Evil communist, you've been hiding like a rat!" Rassoul closes his eyes and reopens them, hoping the nightmarish visions will disappear. But it is no good—they're still here. And you are no longer dreaming, Rassoul. Defend yourself! Do something!

What?

Reassure them, tell them you're not a communist, that these Russian books are not communist propaganda but the works of Dostoevsky. Shout!

"The Russians fucked your mother!" yells one of the armed men as he splits Rassoul's lip with a book. Blood streams.

Forget Dostoevsky! Try something else, beg, swear in the name of Allah.

He tries, but the name of Allah will no longer sing in his throat.

One of the men smacks him even harder, and shoves him to the ground. Rassoul notices then that Yarmohamad is standing in the doorway, watching the scene with a degree of pleasure. One of the men demands: "How long has he been hiding?" Yarmohamad moves closer to reply obsequiously: "Over a year . . . I swear I only rented him the room out of friendship for his cousin, the pious and upright mujahideen Razmodin. I swear to Allah he's been hiding these books from his cousin, too. Razmodin isn't the sort of person to act as guarantor for an ungodly communist, not even his own brother . . ." Sickened, Rassoul tries to protest; he stands up to throw himself on Yarmohamad, grab him by the throat, thump him, bring him back to his senses. Have some self-respect, Yarmohamad! But a sudden kick in the groin crumples him in two. "Trying to escape?"

Escape? No . . . "Why did you break the window?" The window? No, it's . . . Confused, Rassoul clambers painfully to his feet to look out at the courtyard, where everything is dark and silent. He is completely bewildered. His distraught gaze returns to Yarmohamad, to his clean, empty hands.

"Right, you're coming to the police station with us!" They take him, along with a few Russian books as evidence.

As he passes Yarmohamad, Rassoul stares at him, to indicate that he will be paying dearly for this cowardice. He hears him mutter: "Razmodin's going to fuck you up too, for these damned books!"

There's no way these two guys have come round to my place at this time of night to beat me up on account of my books. Someone must have tipped them off about the murder of the old woman. It's all over! The woman in the sky-blue chador, that's who it was. She's finished me. But I'm going to tell, too. I'm going to turn her in as my accomplice. She has no right to live in peace, not sharing my crime and my punishment!

HAVE I fallen asleep again?

And this silence—broken from time to time by the sound of whisperings, muffled footsteps, stifled cries—am I dreaming it?

Open your eyes, and you'll know.

He quickly opens his eyes, but a white light blinds him. He shuts them again and opens them gently. Still the same light. He listens. Still the same sounds. So it isn't a dream?

No. Of that, he can be sure. The bright light, the white walls, the stifled cries all make him feel as if he's in a hospital . . . Except that he isn't in a white bed. He's lying almost flat on an old leather sofa, with a hole in his memory that he tries to repair with the images and sounds that bombard him: the two men attacking him in his bedroom; the door of the "Ministry of Information and Culture"; the blinding beam of light from the guard who stopped them; the two men leading him up the stairs; the shooting pain in his ankle; a long corridor lit by dim bulbs with young, wounded men dozing in corners while others smoked on chairs or decrepit old sofas; further on more men, sitting on the floor around a tablecloth, eating bread and cheese; even further, three or four men cleaning ancient Russian guns; an old man reciting the Koran; another cooking on a portable stove, filling the room with an oily, spicy smell . . . Rassoul is suddenly filled with a strange and distressing sensation, as if he has experienced this scene before. As if he has always been walking up and down this endless corridor under the intent and suspicious gazes of these men. He passes out. Everything goes black.

Now he is here, sitting opposite a most serious-looking man behind a large desk, who is leafing through his Russian books and reading the papers he finds inside them; behind him, the two bearded guards who brought him here.

Rassoul sits up, attracting the attention of the man behind the desk. He seems calm, with a *pakol* on his head and a pointy, weather-beaten face and neatly trimmed beard. He stops reading and asks Rassoul with a slight smile: "Where are you from, *watandar*?"

Watandar—now there's a comforting word, a pretty expression almost forgotten since the start of this fratricidal war. These days, people don't tend to call anyone "countryman" unless they're on the same side. Nothing to fear, then!

And in fact, there isn't anything to fear. I will sit nicely on this sofa, and reply most calmly that I am from Kabul.

His lips move. The name of his hometown is just a

breath, muffled, inaudible. 'I can't hear you,' says the man, leaning over the desk.

Has he already forgotten that his voice doesn't work?

An internal cough to clear his throat, but still not the slightest sound.

Horrified, he starts waving his hands, gesturing, pointing to his Adam's apple, grabbing it between his fingers, just to demonstrate that he is unable to speak. "Are you mute?" No, he gestures. "Can you hear me?" Yes. "Are you ill?" Mmm, yes.

The man leans back in his chair and stares at Rassoul suspiciously for a while, then asks: "Which side are you on?"

"None!" breathes Rassoul, but the word is imprisoned in his vocal cords, and his hands flap about all over the place to communicate the word. The man stands up and holds out a pencil, which he takes to write: *None*. The man reads it. Then he stares at Rassoul again, probably asking himself how it is possible to live in this war-torn land without belonging to any side.

"What tribe are you from?"

Rassoul scribbles: *Born in Kabul*. That is all. The man doesn't seem convinced.

"Where did you learn Russian?"

Rassoul writes: *I was a student in Russia*. The man reads his response aloud, then asks: "And what were you studying?"

Law, writes Rassoul, adding, after a short hesitation: *And to read this damned Dostoevsky!*

43

The man reads, laughs, and asks: "Why *damned* Dostoevsky?" Rassoul shrugs wearily, and points to his bloodstained shirt.

"These two *watandars* are illiterate. For them all Russian books are bound to be propaganda," the man says.

It's OK, Rassoul, you have been saved. This man understands you. You mustn't miss this chance to find out more about why you were arrested. But where to start? Has he read Dostoevsky?

He writes it down. The man reads and replies: "Yes, I read his books when I was a student, in Persian of course. I was studying at the polytechnic. But after the 1981 protests against the Soviet invasion, I abandoned my studies to join the mujahideen. And you—were you in the . . . Komsomol?" He is shrewd, shrewder than he looks. He won't let himself be interrogated by a young Kabuli like you. Don't play with him. Right now, your life is in his hands. He can destroy you with a single breath. Don't be arrogant. Present your life simply and humbly: you spent a few years in Russia, in Leningrad . . . No, better call it Saint Petersburg. Speak about your setbacks, the conflict with your communist father who sent you to study in the USSR against your will. You only stayed three years, from '86 to '89. Over there, you knew a girl whom you called *Kissenka*, poppet. No, don't mention the love affair with a Russian girl. This mujahideen wouldn't approve of that kind of thing with an unbeliever. Just write that you met a

44

Dostoevsky scholar who gave you an initial book, *Crime and Punishment*, which changed your life. You gave it all up . . .

No! That's far too long to write. You have to be concise, precise.

He starts describing his life, but has barely written the first sentence when he is interrupted by the man's rich and thoughtful voice. He is reading aloud from one of the handwritten pages—Rassoul's translated passages from *Crime and Punishment*—and stops to say that he read *The Devils* a long time ago, but not this book. Rassoul leaps up and rummages through his papers to find his translation of the back cover of *Crime and Punishment*. He finds it and gives it to the man, who takes it and reads into his beard: *"The founding act of the novel is the student Raskolnikov's murder of an old moneylender, in her flat in Saint Petersburg. Raskolnikov's reflection on the motive for his crime, plus the influence of Sonia or a mysterious inner impulse, leads him to hand himself in and freely agree to punishment. It is during his years of hard labor that he becomes aware of his love for Sonia, and the path to redemption."* He nods his head in admiration, then says out loud: "An excellent lesson for murderers." Rassoul bites his lips, these lips that move in vain, unable to express the thousand things he has to say about the book. He would like to explain, for the hundredth time, the motives of that murder: it was not only for robbery—to Raskolnikov, the moneylender is an evil beast who steals from people in desperate straits, and therefore killing her is an act of justice; by doing it, Raskolnikov claims his membership of a race of superior beings who exist "beyond good and evil"; for him, his murder is the supreme transgression of the moral and social code, and strikes a blow for independence and freedom, like all the great men in history— Mohammed, Napoleon . . .

What a shame!

". . . It looks like an interesting book. A mystical story," persists the man seriously. And Rassoul continues to curse his muteness, his inability to explain that indeed Dostoevsky is not a revolutionary or a communist, but a mystic. He has said this countless times, but his Russian lecturers would never agree; they didn't approve of that sort of eastern interpretation. And in any case, they couldn't stand Dostoevsky. In Russia, the communists hated him. They wouldn't accept that Dostoevsky's thought went beyond individual psychology to dwell on the metaphysical. This book is best read in Afghanistan, a land previously steeped in mysticism, where people have lost their sense of responsibility. Rassoul is convinced that teaching it here would decrease the number of murders!

What naivety!

Forget Dostoevsky, save yourself, pay attention to this man who is saying to you: "As soon as you get your voice back, come and see me and we'll discuss all this in a civilized manner."

OK, nods Rassoul, lethargically.

"My boys won't give you any more trouble," says the man, gathering up the books. Then he looks curiously at Rassoul, remembering something: "There is one thing that intrigues me."

What?

"Jano tells me that when they came in, you tried to run away. Why?"

No, he didn't want to run away, honestly. He was having a nightmare. The door and the window were jammed shut and he was unable to open them. Look how he has injured his hands.

But who would believe that you can smash a window while dreaming?

The man stares at the hands Rassoul holds out to him. He says, sorrowfully, "We're trying to create order in this neighborhood. But it isn't easy, and disarming the population is not enough. You take their guns, and they start using knives and axes . . . Someone was killed with an ax just yesterday, in broad daylight." That's it, they have discovered Nana Alia's body. And here am I, the murderer, talking with the head of security for the whole city!

Rassoul goes pale. He collapses on the sofa.

"What's the matter, *watandar*?"

Shaken, Rassoul stares at the man with trembling lips. "You look tired. Take your books and go home. You can chat with me another day." He winks at Rassoul, picks up his gun and walks over to wake Jano and the

47

other guard. "Right boys, take this young man back home!" Then to Rassoul, "What is your name?"

Rassoul writes it down.

"Rassoul, we need educated people like you, to serve the nation and Islam. Come and sign up tomorrow, help us to make this neighborhood safe. You come from here. You know everyone's business, everyone's past. You know who lives in each house, and what goes on inside it . . ." He smiles with disarming courtesy as he heads toward the door, then turns back to Rassoul: "Come in and ask for Parwaiz; that's my name." And he is gone. The sly fox! He must know everything. But what does he want from me?

"Come on, Rassoulovski, let's go!" orders a sleepy Jano. Rassoul doesn't move. "Don't you want to go home?"

B EFORE ENTERING the courtyard of his house, Rassoul wishes for just two things: first, that there won't be any blood under the tree (he's still nervous about his nightmare); second, that he won't see Yarmohamad—he doesn't want to dirty his hands with the festering blood of the man he hates, death would be a blessing to someone like that. He must insinuate his way into his life, haunt his soul, enter his dreams, become his fate.

So in he walks, carrying his books. In the moonlit night, he approaches the tree and runs his hand over its trunk. He bends down to check the ground beneath it. No trace of blood. He straightens and looks up at his bedroom window. The glass really is smashed. Then he turns toward Yarmohamad's window. After a brief hesitation, he walks over and shouts that he is back, safe and sound. His cry sticks in his throat. So he raps on the window. Yarmohamad's shaved head looms up out of the darkness. His face is crumpled with sleep and he tells Rassoul to quiet down so as not to wake his wife and children. A waste of time—Rassoul keeps banging on the window. Then he waves his books, and gives Yarmohamad the finger. After that, he turns away and heads to his room. Relieved, and triumphant.

Go on, Yarmohamad, sleep now if you can, the nightmares will come for you this time! I will haunt your dreams.

Once in his room, he feels like shouting. Shouting with joy. Or horror. He exhales forcefully, hoping to summon a noise from his throat. But nothing comes out. Just breath—which burns, but expresses neither joy nor horror.

Cold sweat runs down his back. He throws the books on the ground and lights a candle. The broken window is the thing that interests him most; he still can't understand how he managed to smash it in his sleep.

Have I gone mad? Don't they say that the first sign of madness is when nightmares start breaking out of your sleep to penetrate waking life and take up residence there?

Despairing, he removes his shoes and lies down. He is afraid to close his eyes. Afraid of nightmares. Yes, it is these bed devils, these shadowy figures of the night that are stealing my voice and driving me mad. I will sleep no more!

But his exhaustion is greater than his will. It closes his eyes and pushes him into the depths of darkness. Only the nearby explosion of a rocket rescues him. He starts, and sits up sweating. His tongue is still dry, his chest burning.

Silence, again.

*　　*　　*

The mountain engulfs the moon.
   The night consumes the candle.
   The darkness dulls the room.

Rassoul stands up. Sticks a new candle onto the corpse of the old one, drinks some water, and returns to bed. He doesn't want to lie down anymore. He sits up against the wall. What shall he do? Read a book. He leans over and picks one at random but then tosses it aside and rummages for the first volume of *Crime and Punishment*, which he opens at the page where Raskolnikov returns home after the murder . . .

> *So he lay a very long while. Now and then he seemed to wake up, and at such moments he noticed that it was far into the night, but it did not occur to him to get up. At last he noticed that it was beginning to get light. He was lying on his back, still dazed from his recent oblivion. Fearful, despairing cries rose shrilly from the street, sounds that he heard every night, indeed, under his window after two o'clock. They woke him up now.*
>
> *"Ah! The drunken men are coming out of the taverns," he thought, "it's past two o'clock," and at once he leaped up, as though someone had pulled him from the sofa.*
>
> *"What! Past two o'clock!"*
>
> *He sat down on the sofa—and instantly*

recollected everything! All at once, in one flash,
he recollected everything.

For the first moment he thought he was going
mad. A dreadful chill came over him; but . . .

The cold isn't coming from outside. No, the weather isn't cold at all. Rather it's a chill, a strange kind of chill from inside the room. It is emanating from the faded walls, the blackened, rotting beams . . .

He stands, walks over to the window and opens it. What a beautiful day it is, outside! He puts on his shoes and rushes out of the room, down the stairs and across the courtyard, managing to avoid his landlord. Now he's in the street. Heart leaping and body light, he heads for the river. All around, women, men, young people, musicians are strolling in the afternoon sun. He wanders among them on the banks of the Neva River. No one notices him. No one looks at him suspiciously. And yet he must stand out, in these worn, bloodstained clothes. What joy to go unnoticed, to be imperceptible! Enchanted by the thrill of invisibility, he suddenly, among the crowd, spots a woman in a sky-blue chador. What is she doing here, in Saint Petersburg? She passes him at great speed. He stares at her, confounded. He knows that walk. She disappears into the crowd. He soon pulls himself together and rushes after her. He spots her crossing a busy junction in her chador. He starts sprinting, until he comes close enough to reach out and touch her. He manages to grab hold of her chador and pull it off. The woman is naked. Appalled, she curls into a ball to hide her body and face, but also the object she holds in her hands. Then, slowly, she looks up. It is Sophia. Between her knees is Nana Alia's jewelry box. Confused, Rassoul looks at her and murmurs something inaudible. Then he shuts his eyes and throws himself at her feet to cry out in thanks. He feels saved. She has saved him. A hand is shaking him. "Rassoul! Rassoul!" It is not Sophia's voice. It's a man's voice. A man he knows. Razmodin, his cousin. But where is he?

Here, in front of you, in your room. Open your eyes!

Barely awake, Rassoul scrambles to his feet, knocking the copy of *Crime and Punishment* off his chest. "Razmodin?" His cousin's name trembles on his lips and is lost. He coughs and pretends to say "Salam." Razmodin, who is crouching nearby, looks at him anxiously.

"Are you all right, cousin?"

Rassoul opens his eyes wide, then closes them again thoughtfully. Razmodin insists. "What's going on? Are you well?"

Rassoul nods his head and sits down on the mattress, gazing at the broken window. It is already day but the sky is still black, black with smoke. "Do you want me to take you to a doctor?" No, it's OK, he gestures. "Yes, I can see that! Tell me what's going on!" Razmodin's worried gaze lingers on Rassoul's shirt. "What is that blood? Did they beat you up?"

After a moment's thought, Rassoul stands up to look

out at the courtyard, and sees Yarmohamad watching him. He beckons him to come up. But the landlord goes back inside his own house. "Leave him alone! He came to my office at dawn and told me everything. He was pale and kept telling me it wasn't him . . . And that's the truth. There are patrols everywhere, these days. Especially in this neighborhood . . . You've no idea what's going on in this country right now. Buried in who-knows-what world, you have no interest . . ." Stop, Razmodin, please! Look what they've done to him.

Razmodin stops, not to notice the state Rassoul is in, but to hear him explain himself. He waits a moment. Nothing. He can't believe it. Rassoul rolls up his sleeves to reveal his bruises. "What sons of bitches! But you're a madman, too. What are you doing with all these Russian books in times like this?" Rassoul's ankle starts hurting again. He grimaces and sits back down on the bed to rub it. His cousin stares down at him. "Dostoevsky! Dostoevsky! You're always getting in trouble with your damned Dostoevsky! How do you expect them to know who he is?"

They aren't all as ignorant as you, Razmodin! Commandant Parwaiz, whose name I'm sure you know, is very familiar with Dostoevsky. His troops are based just opposite your place, in the Ministry of Culture and Information. But in my current state, I am not able to tell you about it.

Write it down!

What's the point? It's more peaceful like this, without

words, without all these endless conversations. I'll just leave him to wonder at my mute state.

"Yarmohamad told me that they took you to Commandant Parwaiz's office. I know him." So you were right. "We were imprisoned together during the 1979 protests. That was a stroke of luck, being sent to him. Did you mention my name?" Rassoul shakes his head, then stands up to lurk behind the window once more. Yarmohamad is back in the courtyard. Rassoul beckons again for him to come over. "Forget him, it's done. I paid him the two months' rent you owed, he'll leave you alone now." Distressed by his cousin's generosity, Rassoul totters back to his bed and attempts to communicate in sign language that he shouldn't have done it, that he, Rassoul, would have paid it . . . The same words he'd used last time, when Razmodin paid three months' rent on his behalf.

"And what exactly would you have paid it with?! You've let everything drop. Look at the state of you. You look like a beggar, or a madman escaped from an asylum!" Razmodin would have said, again.

So there is no point in Rassoul going to such lengths to make himself understood. But Razmodin expects to hear it from Rassoul. He can't understand why he won't talk to him. He looks on curiously as Rassoul stands up and rummages through a mound of clothing, looking for a clean shirt. They are all dirty and rumpled. Rassoul knows that. He is just pretending, so he doesn't have to respond to Razmodin. The thing is, he doesn't want him to know that he has lost his voice. They are cousins, and know each other well. They can hear each other's thoughts, even when they are unspoken. Despite this, Razmodin insists as he always does.

"Rassoul, you've got to do something. How long are you going to live like this? If I could speak the languages you can, I'd have earned buckets of cash by now. These foreign journalists and humanitarian organizations are all crying out for interpreters. Every day, a hundred times a day, people ask me if I know someone who speaks even a little English. But how can I give them your name? You've already landed me in the shit. I've regretted it a dozen times." And again, he will forgive him. "If you want, you can put the past behind you and start again. But I beg you, cousin, stop being so aggressive with the journalists. What business is it of yours who works for who, or why they are defending this or that group? Just take the dollars—fuck them and their ideas and shitty political posturing!" But this time, he doesn't wait for Rassoul to bend his ear with his usual motto: "I'd rather be a murderer than a traitor!" Instead, he continues: "It's easy to say that you'd rather be a murderer than a traitor. Why don't you carry a gun then? You're burying your head in the sand. If you're asked to fly, you say you're a camel, and if you're asked to carry, you say you're a bird. You've dropped your parents, forgotten your sister and your friends. If you want to fuck everything up then just carry on as you are. Do you even know what you want from life?" Furious, he stands up, takes a cigarette from his pocket and lights it. Despite his annoyance at these repeated reproaches, Rassoul is still pretending to look for a shirt, while nodding his head and drawing circles in the air with his hand to signal that he knows what's coming.

"I swear, you've changed, you're no longer the same man. You wanted Sophia, you got her. But what are you doing with her now? Do you want her to meet the same fate as you? We grew up together, cousin, we know each other, you're like my brother. You taught me everything . . ." Razmodin doesn't finish the sentence, because when he made the same speech—or nearly—a few weeks ago, Rassoul snapped: "Except for one thing."

"What?"

"The horror of a moral lecture."

"I'm not trying to lecture you. I'm holding up a mirror."

"A mirror? No, it's the bottom of a glass that bears only your own face, and which you hold up to others in order to say *Be like me!*"

Better to shut up, Razmodin. You think I'm pretending not to give a fuck about what you're telling me. It's a good thing you don't know that I'm condemned to silence, or you'd still be speaking. You'd have emptied out your heart, bilious from my previous insults, without hearing me say that I don't want your charity, I don't like your fleamarket humanitarians, I hate these philanthropists who only care about their own name, I can't stand all these buzzards circling above our corpses, these

57

flies buzzing around the arsehole of a dead cow. Yes, I hate everything now: myself, and you too, my cousin, my childhood friend—you who are looking into my eyes, waiting for me to say something. Well, you won't hear anything from me now. Perhaps you think this silence is a sign of indifference toward you. Or else resignation to your recriminations.

Interpret it how you will. What difference will that make to the world? To me? None. So just leave me alone!

After this long silence, Razmodin attacks again: "So now you won't speak to me anymore? It's all over?" Rassoul stops rummaging through his clothes. He shrugs his shoulders to show that he has nothing left to say. Disappointed, Razmodin stands up. "You've really lost it now, Rassoul. If you don't want to see me anymore, or listen to me, then I'm off . . . ," he heads toward the door . . . "the fact that I paid the rent was just to protect our family's honor. That's it!" and he leaves.

Rassoul is dumbfounded, his face frozen. Then suddenly he rushes to the window to cry out.

I can no longer even yell my despair, my hatred, my rage . . .

So cry out in hope, joy, serenity. Perhaps that will help you find your voice again.

Where must I look for them?

Wherever you lost them.

R ASSOUL LOOKS at himself in the small mirror hanging from the wall; looks with rage and hatred. He strokes his beard. He moistens his cheeks with the last drops of water from the jug, and picks up his razor; the blade is blunt; he continues regardless; it grazes his skin. The blood flows. He takes no notice, shaving furiously, scraping the blade repeatedly across and under his chin. A fly starts buzzing around the cuts. He waves it away. It comes back and tastes the blood. He slaps it away harshly, making the razor slip on his cheek. Another cut. He doesn't give a damn. He keeps shaving, more and more frantic, as if trying to scrape off his skin.

His movements are slowed by the sound of footsteps on the stairs. Someone knocks at the door. After a moment of stillness and silence he opens without bothering to wipe his bloodstained face. It is a woman in a sky-blue chador. When she sees Rassoul she gives a muffled cry and steps back slightly. Then she unveils herself. Sophia. Her innocent eyes are wide with horror. "What happened, Rassoul?" He runs his hand over his face, moving his lips to indicate that it's just the blunt blade . . . but she doesn't understand. "What's the matter?" Nothing, gestures Rassoul, despairingly. "We waited up late for you last night. Why didn't you come? My mother was so worried. She didn't sleep all night." Should I explain to her that I've lost my voice? Yes, why not. Who else can you confide in?

Rassoul takes a step backward into the room, so Sophia can enter. Then he starts looking for a pen and paper. But Sophia notices Yarmohamad's children watching and decides to remain at the door. "I don't want to bother you. I just came to find you to go . . ." She doesn't finish her sentence, perturbed by Rassoul rummaging anxiously through his books. After a moment of silence and hesitation, she pulls the chador back down over her face and departs, leaving Rassoul to search for something on which to write his voiceless words, leaving him in that dream where he's pursuing her through the streets of Saint Petersburg. And what if that woman in the sky-blue chador really was her? A stupid question that forces him into action. He rushes down to the courtyard. Sophia is already out on the street. He washes his face at the courtyard tap, returns to his room to change, and sets off after her.

What an absurd thought! If it had been Sophia, you would have recognized her voice.

Her voice?

He stops.

Don't tell me you don't know her voice!

Of course I know it, but I can't remember how it

sounds when she shouts. Actually, I've never heard her shout, or raise her voice at all. Well, what about her walk? The way she runs?

Sophia moves as if in water. Her shoulders move back and forth like fins. Yes, but that particular way of walking was a long time ago, without a chador. All women walk the same in the chador, don't they?

They do.

Uncertainty and doubt make Rassoul limp even faster on his way to Sophia's house. He is so bizarrely over-excited that he cannot convince himself such a shy and innocent girl would never get up to something as dangerous as that.

It was her, he feels like yelling at the top of his voice. Her! She did it, not only out of love for me and her family, but also from hate for Nana Alia! Yes! She did it!

As he weaves through the crowded streets, engulfed in the black smoke that has descended on the city, a man grabs him by the shoulder, stopping him in his tracks.

"Rassoulovski?"

It is Jano's cheerful voice. Jano notices the cuts on Rassoul's face. "Did we do that to you?" No, he mimes, a razor. The blade of destiny, he would have said if he still had his voice. "You lucky devil! At least you know you have a destiny," Jano would probably have replied. A destiny. Rassoul would rather not have one at all.

"And your voice?"

Still nothing.

After a few steps in silence, Jano asks: "So, are you going to join Commandant Parwaiz? He'll give you a good Kalashnikov! Do you know how to shoot?" No. "You'll learn it all in a day. In any case . . ." he leans in close, whispers, "the bullet finds its own target," and he laughs. A brief, smug laugh followed by a wink at the Kalashnikov he keeps hidden beneath his *patou*.

Another few steps in silence. They are both thinking— Rassoul about the slow blade of his destiny, Jano about the targets of his stray bullets. They come to a *chaikhana,* and the young soldier invites Rassoul in. Why not? He feels like something to eat and drink, and more importantly getting to know Parwaiz's crew, finding out whether or not they've found Nana Alia's corpse. In brief, there are a thousand reasons to pursue this adventure instead of trying to find Sophia.

Inside they sit by a window, next to three armed men who immediately break off their conversation to stare.

Jano orders tea and bread. Apropos of nothing, he asks Rassoul: "Your landlord . . . do you know him well?" Yes, Rassoul nods sadly. Jano continues, "When we came into the house yesterday evening, just on patrol, he rushed over to tell us about his strange ex-communist tenant who had stopped paying his rent . . ." Rassoul's persistent silence prevents Jano from continuing. He glances anxiously at their neighbors, who are still staring. How annoying. He takes a noisy gulp of tea and goes on.

"Your blade scratches your face. Ours is sharper, it injures our very souls!" He stuffs a piece of bread into his mouth. "I was only twelve when the war broke out. My father put a gun on my shoulder and sent me off to do jihad against the Red Army. The things I saw . . . If you were in my shoes, you wouldn't want to hear a single word of Russian, my friend. They burned down our village. I found my family's remains, burnt to ashes! Commandant Parwaiz adopted me. He gave me the strength and courage to fight to avenge my family. And while we were mourning our dead, the destruction of our villages, the humiliation of our sisters . . . you, you were having a grand old time in the arms of little blonde white girls, soft and lively as fish . . . isn't that right?" Another gulp of scalding tea. "You never imagined that we starving, barefoot creatures could ever take power . . ." Rassoul painfully ingests both the bread and the words. Even the tea burns his throat, his tongue. He would like to respond that his life hasn't been as peaceful as Jano might think. By telling him about his conflict with his communist father, he might make himself more sympathetic.

No guarantee of that. Jano would probably reproach him in much the same way as another mujahideen he'd spoken to recently: "That too is your Russian education."

"What do you mean?"

"Not respecting your father is a Russian abomination!"

"But I didn't want to follow my father's ideology. I was against the invasion of my country by the Russians."

"If you were a good son, you would respect him and follow his path, his beliefs!"

"But what are you saying? How can one follow a father who is a war criminal?"

"That's right, you must never betray your father, not even if he's a murderer."

"And if he's an unbeliever?"

Silence.

Jano sips his tea, his chest puffed out. Rassoul watches him, holding on to his rage and his desire to crush it against this chest puffed up with arrogant, rotten pride, to destroy this cage stuffed with hollow power . . .

But why, Rassoul? What do you know about him? He hasn't said anything. Leave the guy alone. He is happy. He is proud. He isn't suffering as you are. Thank God that you can't speak!

Drink your tea, eat your bread, and get out of here!

As Rassoul stands up, one of the armed men addresses Jano. "Excuse me, brother, aren't you Jano?"

"Yes."

The man walks up to him, smiling. "Don't you recognize me? Momène, from Commandant Nawroz's troop?"

Jano drops his glass of tea, startled. "Of course! How could I forget? You've changed a bit. Put on weight, definitely! That must be five or six years ago . . . or more?"

"Six years."

They stand up, throw themselves into each other's

arms, embrace warmly, and sit back down together. The perfect chance for Rassoul to escape. He gets to his feet to shake Jano's hand and take his leave. But the soldier won't have it. He invites him to drink another tea with these old friends.

"Sit down!" He turns toward the other men. "Last night we beat this brother during a patrol, and today we're drinking tea together! Who says we don't want peace!" He snorts with laughter, tugging at Rassoul to sit down.

And Rassoul complies.

They order more tea. And smoke cigarettes. Momène starts telling his friends about "Our unforgettable operation! Six years ago . . ."

"Yes, six years ago," confirms Jano nostalgically. He turns to Rassoul. "It was summertime. A summer evening. We were on our way to attack a Soviet location. We'd been told that Commandant Nawroz would be in charge of this operation. Commandant Nawroz and our Commandant Parwaiz didn't get on at all, but they decided to attack the Russians together anyway. We would take the prisoners, and they would get the guns . . ." Interrupted by a laugh from Momène, he takes a gulp of tea then continues. "Anyway, as soon as night fell we attacked!" This time he's interrupted by his own laughter, and it is Momène who takes up the story.

"In our regiment there was a mujahideen by the name of Shirdel. A brave man and a good Muslim, but with a soft spot for the boys! So we nicknamed him *Kirdel*—lover of cock." At this, everybody fell about laughing. "When our troop silently and carefully attacked the weapons depot, our *bradar* Shirdel came across a young Russian soldier taking a shit!" Their loud laughter silences everyone in the tearoom. They start listening, too. Jano is laughing so hard there are tears streaming down his face. Momène continues: "Imagine our Shirdel in such a situation! His heart was beating a hundred miles an hour; he didn't know what to do; he was trembling with fear that a mujahideen would shoot this dreamy creature with the smooth white buttocks! Anyway, he captured him and, once the operation had been carried out successfully, took him to Commandant Nawroz, who ordered that he be given to Commandant Parwaiz. But who was he telling! Shirdel immediately handcuffed himself to the pretty boy and swallowed the key!"

They all roar with laughter. Rassoul does too, but deep inside. When the laughter quiets down, Jano continues: "Commandant Parwaiz took them both. He talked to Shirdel at great length, but he wouldn't listen. He had changed. It was all over for him—jihad, prayer . . . They walked around together from morning till night, hand in hand. Shirdel sang for him, taught him our language . . . And then one night, they disappeared." He turns to Momène. "You never saw them again?"

"No, never," replies Momène, wiping away his tears. "What a time!"

66

"Exactly, what a time! We may not have seen eye to eye, but against the Russians we were united!"

"We were!"

"And now look, these days we're fighting each other. Why?"

"Ask Commandant Nawroz!"

"And you, ask your Commandant Parwaiz!"

The laughter stops.

A silent hatred invades the *chai-khana*.

Rassoul stands up, gestures quietly at Jano—who waves goodbye—and makes a speedy exit.

He has barely reached the end of the road when he is startled by two gunshots, fired not far behind.

In the *chai-khana?*

Perhaps.

He stops, turns around.

Let them kill each other!

He continues on his way to Sophia's house.

H E KNOCKS at the gate and waits. The fearful voice of Sophia's mother: "Who is it?" Hearing no response, she repeats her question. "It's Rassoul!" cries Sophia's brother, Dawoud, who is perched on the roof of the house.

The mother opens the gate, sees Rassoul's cut face, and shivers. "What happened to you?" Nothing, I just cut myself shaving, that's all, he would have liked to reply, not bothering to elaborate on the blade of destiny. But he just mimes what happened and comes inside, as the mother complains: "You were supposed to come yesterday evening. I didn't get a wink of sleep." He nods as if to say that he knows. Too bad if he can't apologize.

The mother peers into the empty lane for someone else and, stunned to see Rassoul alone, demands: "Where is Sophia?"—Didn't she come home? Rassoul asks with his eyes. "Isn't she with you?" No. Rassoul's shaking head makes her still more anxious. She glances into the lane, then turns back toward him, leaving the gate open in the hope her daughter will suddenly appear. "She wanted you to go with her to Nana Alia's, to do her books . . ." To Nana Alia's! He leans against the wall to stop himself staggering. "She told me that you'd asked her to break ties with the old woman. Then two days ago, her daughter Nazigol came here to tell me that if Sophia no longer wanted to work for her, she would first have to pay the outstanding rent. We waited for you all yesterday, to discuss it. When you didn't come, she went, but . . ." She too went there yesterday? ". . . Nana Alia wasn't there." She wasn't there? What about her body? "Sophia wanted to go back today. I asked her to take you with her." Take me? "Weren't you at home?"

I was. So why didn't she say anything? Look at the state you're in, Rassoul. No one would dare ask you for anything these days. Your unexplained and incomprehensible silence gives the impression that everyone upsets you.

"I worry so much for Sophia, Rassoul. Take care of her. Don't leave us like this, all alone and without news of you. In these times, young girls are disappearing. The warlords raid the city to take them for their wives." Her voice is broken by a sob. But Rassoul is no longer listening. His legs wobble. It seems as if the floor is giving way, collapsing beneath his feet. He leans on the wall and lets himself slide to the ground. The mother continues: "And that blasted Nana Alia is worse than the warlords. I'm afraid she will hurt Sophia." She sits down facing Rassoul. "My late husband placed us in your hands; aside from you we have no one. And you . . ."

But he is walled in by silence, gripped by the continuing mystery surrounding the murder of blasted Nana Alia, lost in his suspicions about the woman in the sky-blue chador who, in his fantasies, can only be Sophia. He must find her!

He stands up and leaves. On the way,

He catches no eye,

Hears no voice,

Smells no aroma,

Feels no pain.

He runs.

Runs as if his ankle no longer hurt.

But his foot has not forgotten. It twists, and stops him in his tracks. Stops him not far from Nana Alia's house, on the corner of her street, where the same black dog is still lying in the shadow of the wall. This time, the idle dog is more alert and stands up, rushes at him, chases him away. Rassoul cannot enter that house as if nothing had happened there.

Nothing did happen. Look! Listen! This silence, this stillness gives no indication of mourning.

So, perhaps the stroke of the ax was not fatal. She escaped alive. She must be in the hospital by now. She can't be conscious yet, or I would be behind bars.

He is sweating, the sweat of fear. He must leave this place, return to Sophia's house and wait for her there. But his legs are heavy, bogged down in the ground, as if they want him to stay here and settle this.

Yes, it must be settled.

Sooner or later, Nana Alia will tell.

Sooner or later, you will pay.

So why not today, right here and now, at the scene of the crime?

He walks up to the half-open gate, pushes it gently, and peers into the courtyard. The house is completely calm and quiet. Just a few hens pecking and clucking. He walks up to the house and to the terrace steps. The air is heavy, the silence dense, his footsteps uncertain. He stops to peek through the windows. Not a soul behind the curtains. He is trembling with curiosity and fear. Sweat hangs on his forehead, and he has to hold on to the wall to make it up the steps. On reaching the terrace he jumps—a silhouette has appeared, finally, in the darkness of the corridor. "Rassoul? Is that you?" asks Sophia's voice. Rassoul panics and tries to speak, forgetting his muteness; his lips move in vain to explain that he has come to find her, that her mother is very worried. It makes Sophia laugh. "What's the matter with you? I couldn't hear a word," she says, moving closer. Rassoul freezes as he sees another silhouette emerge from the corridor behind Sophia. It is Nazigol.

"Nana Alia disappeared yesterday. No one knows where she is . . ." exclaims Sophia.

Rassoul stares at Nazigol, not knowing what to do, or think, or say. Nana Alia is no longer here. That's the only thing they know. How should he receive this news? Should he be glad? Or suspicious?

Nazigol takes a step closer. "When I came yesterday evening, no one was in. My mother never goes out without leaving someone here, especially in the evening." Rassoul stares at the two girls, increasingly stunned and increasingly secretive.

Nazigol turns to Sophia. "When I found the house empty, I was afraid to stay here alone. I closed all the doors and left . . ." Her voice tapers off. All sound fades. Rassoul can no longer hear anything, or see anything. There is just a hole, a black hole, the corridor, silent and morbid, a deep, endless abyss with no way out.

He staggers dumbly into the house, and Nana Alia's fat body appears on the stairs at the end of the corridor. He says hello. She asks him what he wants. The smoke from her cigarette, caught in a ray of light, obscures her face. Rassoul walks along the passage and holds out a watch that he promised her the other day. She says she has no more money to pawn it. He begs her, swearing that he will only leave it for a day or two. It is a precious watch, full of jewel bearings. He bought it in Leningrad. He only wants two thousand afghanis. Nana Alia takes a step back, suspicious. She can't understand why Rassoul is wearing a *patou* in this heat. She asks him. He says that he is ill, feverish. She takes the watch and looks at it. The hands say nine minutes past six—it doesn't work.

It does normally work, but the battery has died. Rassoul would have replaced it if he had the cash.

Nonsense! This is an old wind-up watch. It doesn't use batteries! She tries to give it back. He won't take it. He begs her again, just two thousand afghanis. The watch contains twelve precious jewels. Look—it says so on the back.

No, she doesn't want it. Rassoul insists. The watch is Russian, an excellent brand. She can give him whatever she wants, damn it! But the old lady is increasingly suspicious of Rassoul, who is now trembling. He grabs her hand and puts it to his forehead so she can feel how feverish and exhausted he is. He hasn't eaten for two days. She pulls back her hand, hesitates, then agrees to take the watch but on one condition: that he lets his fiancée return to work; otherwise, she will retrieve her money the very next day, and what's more she will kick out his fiancée and her whole family. Rassoul agrees. As soon as he leaves here, he'll go to Sophia and ask her to return to work.

The old lady is about to go, but turns back to tell Rassoul something: from now on it will be she, and she alone, who decides what time Sophia leaves work. He nods.

Then she instructs him to wait in the passage, and heads for the stairs. As soon as she's upstairs Rassoul is on the move—stealthy, anxious and upset. The ax he has hidden beneath his *patou* is becoming more and more burdensome; his arms, weak; his legs, stiff. He struggles to climb the stairs, to reach the upstairs corridor where he sees Nana Alia opening a little door.

After a short hesitation she enters the room and closes the door behind her. Rassoul staggers up to the door. He puts an ear to it and listens to the sound of cupboards being opened and shut. He takes a deep breath, kicks down the door and rushes at Nana Alia, who is counting a wad of notes by the window. The moment Rassoul lifts the ax to bring it down on the old woman's head, the thought of *Crime and Punishment* flashes into his mind. It strikes him to the very core. His arms shake; his legs tremble. And the ax slips from his hands. It splits open the old woman's head, and sinks into her skull. She collapses without a sound on the red and black rug. Her apple-blossom-patterned headscarf floats in the air, before landing on her large, flabby body. She convulses. Another breath; perhaps two. Her staring eyes fix on Rassoul standing in the middle of the room, not breathing, whiter than a corpse. His *patou* falls from his bony shoulders. His terrified gaze is lost in the pool of blood, blood that streams from the old woman's skull, merges with the red of the rug, obscuring its black pattern, then trickles toward the woman's fleshy hand, which still grips a wad of notes. The money will be bloodstained.

Move, Rassoul, move!

"RASSOUL?"

He returns to his senses and turns, panic-stricken, toward the voice. Sophia and Nazigol are standing in the doorway, looking at him in shock. "What's happening to you, Rassoul?" asks Sophia, taking a step toward him. He paces the room, distraught, peering anxiously into every nook and cranny. No trace of his crime.

"Have you been in this room before?" asks Nazigol curiously. "My mother always used to lock it. No one apart from me and her were ever allowed to set foot in here." She turns toward Sophia. "When did you last clean this room?"

"Never. She always cleaned it herself."

Rassoul looks at the window he used to escape. It is closed. He is so shaken that he almost faints. Water! He turns toward Sophia, miming drink. "Yes, wait!" she says, murmuring to Nazigol as she runs out the door, "he's very unwell just now."

Rassoul stares at Nana Alia's daughter as she rummages through the cupboards. More and more curious, she wonders aloud: "Could she have taken all her jewelry with her?" Then she leaves the room to look next door. Sophia comes back with a glass of water and gives it to Rassoul. He drinks. Slowly, not so much for the refreshment as to give himself time to think before Nazigol returns.

How to explain or justify entering the room?

If you could, you'd say that a long time ago, when Nazigol's father was still alive—for this must have been his room—you'd brought him documents from the National Archives belonging to Sophia's father, etc.

Come back, blasted voice!

"Surely she didn't take all her money with her?" wonders Nazigol, looking suspiciously at Rassoul and Sophia. After a moment's heavy silence, Rassoul rushes into the corridor, followed by Sophia. "What's the matter, Rassoul?" Nothing . . . nothing! He waves his hands about as he runs down the stairs. "What's happening to you? Are you OK? You seem so strange," she insists. He stops dead, thinking how to make her understand that he has no voice to tell her what's going on. But Nazigol is following them, she's there, behind Sophia, asking them: "What should I do? Where should I go? I don't know if my mother will come back this evening or not."

"Come on, we'll go to my house."

"No chance, Mother will curse me if she comes back and finds the house deserted. But where on earth has she gone? I'd better go to my uncle's place, and find out if he knows anything . . ." She suddenly looks at Rassoul. "Can you stay here till I get back?"

"OK. Go on, then . . ." replies Sophia, sending Rassoul into a panic. There's no way he can stay here, no way! His eyes say no, confirmed by his hands. But Nazigol begs, and Sophia decides, saying "Go on, go!" and then to Rassoul, "Let her go, that's not nice."

And why are you resisting, Rassoul? Let her go. It will give you time to rummage through the house, and find a clue to help you solve the mystery.

It is Nazigol who is the mystery. She is no innocent in all this. I'm sure of it.

Let her go, then!

Nazigol leaves.

Sophia gazes at Rassoul lovingly, but his mind is elsewhere. He waits for Nazigol's footsteps to fade away down the street. "Where are you going?" cries Sophia, following Rassoul back into the room. "What on earth are you doing?" Rassoul is searching the room. "Don't rummage through their house. That's not nice. If they come back . . ." He gestures at her to go downstairs. More and more upset, she remains at the door. "No, Rassoul, you've no right to do this. Tell me what you're looking for!"

You must respond, Rassoul. You can't get out of this so easily. You've got to tell her everything.

But how? This isn't the time.

She's finding you more and more weird, abstruse . . .

So much the better!

77

What if it that woman in the sky-blue chador really was her?

He stops scouring the room and glares suspiciously at Sophia for a long time, almost aggressively.

"What's the matter? Why are you looking at me like that? Why won't you tell me anything?"

Silence. Staring. Suspicions . . .

She leaves the room, exasperated. He goes back to his rummaging—inside the cupboards, under the table, in the drawers, beneath the sofa . . . No trace of the things he left behind yesterday: no jewelry box, no money, no ax, no *patou*. Nothing. He sits on the rug and runs his hand over the spot where the corpse lay. It is clean and dry. Is this the same rug? Who could have arranged such quick, efficient cleaning? It all seems the work of a professional, not two young girls like Nazigol and Sophia!

Disconcerted, he stands up and is about to leave the room when his gaze falls on a box on top of the wardrobe. He opens it, but finds only six packs of Marlboro cigarettes. He takes one and returns the box. But what about the other five, who is he leaving them for? He takes the lot.

As he passes the half-open door to the kitchen, he spots a plate of food on the table. He walks in, starving, picks up a big handful of sticky rice, and stuffs it into his mouth. It isn't good. He spits it out on the plate. Then he carefully inspects the room. He still doesn't find anything to give him any kind of clue as to what has happened. He grabs the matches that are on the table and leaves. He lights a cigarette, and takes a long drag. Outside, he finds Sophia sitting on the terrace steps, staring at the front gate. Still frightened and furious, she asks: "What's going on? Why won't you say anything?" Rassoul, waving at the air with his hands, tries to express how weary he is of the question. "Lost your tongue, have you?" Yes, he nods, knowing Sophia won't take him seriously. "What were you looking for up there?" He exhales smoke in her direction. "Cigarettes?" He looks at her and sits down, preoccupied. A thousand questions run through his mind. What time did she come here, yesterday? Did she see anyone? It couldn't have been before the murder; otherwise, Nana Alia would have told him she'd come.

No, she can't be the woman in the blue chador. If she was, she would never have agreed to stay in the house.

But she didn't stay to protect the house, or for your sake. She wanted to be alone with you. You've never had that opportunity—a lovers' tête-à-tête! She has a thousand things to tell you. A thousand things she'd like to hear from you . . .

Sophia's loving gaze rests on Rassoul's lips, obscured by a curl of smoke. "You said you didn't want to smoke anymore." He drags harder on his cigarette and blows the smoke into her hair. They laugh.

Sophia's laugh; what a joy! He adores that crystal-clear laugh, innocent and so fragile it falters under the slightest glance, the smallest of movements, but still it lights up her eyes.

The faraway sound of bullets and rockets doesn't disturb the peaceful silence that has settled between them.

Sophia shyly puts her hand on Rassoul's knee, in the hope that he might take it in his, stroke it, that they might delight in this loving moment. But his hands do not move. They are trembling, dripping with sweat.

"Have you decided to stop speaking?" asks Sophia desperately, staring at Rassoul's unmoving lips.

After a short hesitation he jumps to his feet to go into the house, find a pen and paper, and write it all down for her. But he is stopped by a noise at the gate. Someone wants to come in. Is it Nazigol, back already? Rassoul throws down his cigarette and rushes to hide in the darkness of the corridor. Sophia goes to the gate. "Who's there?"

"Nana Alia?" asks a deep, male voice. Sophia, panicking, replies: "No, she isn't here."

"What time will she be back?"

"I don't know."

"Who are you? Nazzi?"

"No, Nazigol isn't here either. I'm their maid."

"No! Sophia . . . ?"

"No . . ."

"Of course it is! Be a sweetie and open up! It's me, Commandant Amer Salam." He pushes hard on the gate, which Sophia struggles to keep closed with her fragile, trembling hands as she cries: "No . . . No, I'm not Sophia . . . they told me not to let anyone in."

"And I'm *anyone*? Come on, open up!" He starts pushing again. Hopeless—Sophia quickly attaches the security chain. Amer Salam shakes the gate even harder.

Rassoul surges out of the darkness to rush at the gate and yank it open. Taken aback, Amer Salam asks loudly: "Isn't Nana Alia in?" No, gestures Rassoul furiously. The commandant peers over his shoulder for Sophia, and says: "Then tell her that Amer Salam will be coming tonight with some guests. There will be seven of us, seven!" And with that he leaves.

Sophia collapses weakly to the ground from her hiding place behind the gate. Rassoul closes it and watches helplessly through the gaps in the wall as Amer Salam wanders back to his car, parked a little way off. Then he moves away, nervously lights a cigarette and goes to sit on one of the terrace steps. Sophia stands up and walks over to him. He stares at her as if to ask *And who is Amer Salam?*

Come on, Rassoul, you love asking questions to which you already know the answer. He must be one of Nana Alia's regular clients, who comes here to watch young dancing girls. Leave Sophia alone.

She puts her head on her knees and weeps, silently. Rassoul, confused, doesn't know whether to comfort her or drive her away.

Why drive her away? She deserves to be comforted, loved, honored.

Tenderly, hesitantly, he puts his hand on her shoulder. She is soothed, as if not expecting this moment of grace. She huddles into his arms and starts sobbing in earnest. Rassoul strokes her back. If he could speak, she would hear him say: "It's all over, Sophia. That dirty whore is gone. I killed her. Calm down!"

She is still crying. She doesn't want to stop. She doesn't stop. She will never stop, not while Rassoul is stroking her. May this moment last forever—these tears, and this stroking!

But sadly, it does end. Rassoul is on edge, not so much because of Sophia as from his strange experience of being in the house. He feels as if someone is watching them from the corridor. He stands and peers angrily behind him. Then he gestures to Sophia to leave right now. "When Nazigol comes back." No, this house is cursed! He runs to the door. "But if they come back and we aren't here, Nana Alia will kick us out of our house."

Nana Alia can go to hell! I've killed her.

He throws his cigarette into the courtyard, opens the gate and runs out into the lane. Sophia, horrified, chases after him. "Rassoul! Do you know what's happened to Nana Alia?" Don't try and find out what he's done to her, Sophia! You will lose him. "What's the matter? I've a right to know." He stops and stares at her, both oppressed and oppressive. How to tell her that she'll find out soon enough, that he himself will explain. "Damn! My chador! Hang on, I'll go back and get it."

She goes. Rassoul continues on his way. After a few steps he stops. The pain in his ankle. He rubs it.

Far away, somewhere in the city, there is a volley of gunshots. He looks up at the Asmai Heights. A group of armed men are climbing to the summit.

He, on the other hand, is going down, toward the *saqi-khana* where . . .

S OMEONE IS coughing—a loose, drawn-out cough. Then they spit. Between coughs we hear a voice; a rich, solemn voice belonging to a certain Kaka Sarwar, reciting: ". . . *and thus Dhul-Qarnayn took a new road toward the north. He came to a city located between two mountains, and there he found a people who spoke some isolated language and could understand no other, and who were suffering the oppression of Gog and Magog, two evil tribes drawn from the dregs of society who were ravaging the area.*" He stops to inhale a lungful of hash. "*Seeing that he was a strong and powerful man, the people asked Dhul-Qarnayn to build a wall between them and the men of Gog and Magog, and offered to give him a handsome tribute in return. Gog and Magog were indeed two wicked and vicious tribes, who would listen to no counsel and feared nothing. As Dhul-Qarnayn was naturally inclined to do good and help the oppressed he immediately agreed to assist this people, but refused any payment in exchange. He said to them: 'That which my Lord has established in me is better than tribute. Help me therefore with strength and labour and I will build a barrier between you and them.'*" Kaka Sarwar pauses again in his tale to gulp some tea. "*Dhul-Qarnayn thus asked the people to bring him blocks of iron, wood, copper, and charcoal. He erected the blocks of iron between the two mountains, and surrounded them with pieces of wood and charcoal. Then he lit the fire, and as soon as it turned into a furnace poured the molten copper on top. And thus Gog and Magog could neither scale nor pierce the wall. When Dhul-Qarnayn had finished, he cried: 'This is a mercy from my Lord. But when the promise of my Lord comes to pass, He will make it into dust. And the promise of my Lord is true!'*"

"Kaka Sarwar, when will this promise come?"

"But it is already come, dear Hakim! It was said that on the day of the apocalypse the hordes of Gog and Magog would make a hole in the barrier, and Allah would allow them to spread over the earth. They would dominate the world and wipe out the human race; then they would condemn Allah to death, by sending arrows up into the sky . . . Where is the chillum?" It is brought to him. He smokes and asks: "Do you know this passage from the Koran?"

"No."

"Shame on you! And do you not know either where this city is to be found?"

"No."

"Shame on you! This city is here, it is Kabul!" A final drag, and he withdraws into a corner. "Kaka Sarwar, don't leave us with this terrible story! Recite us a poem!"

asks a little man sitting next to Rassoul. Eyes closed, Kaka Sarwar sings quietly: "*O City Mufti, you go more astray / Than I do, though to wine I do give way; I drink the blood of grapes, you that of men: / Which of us is the more bloodthirsty, pray?*"

"Me!" says a voice. There is widespread, hollow laughter. Then silence, languor, dreams . . . The world is merely a transparent space without substance or weight. In the middle of it all, Rassoul. Swimming. Naked. Innocent. Weightless and delicate. How he loves this state of grace. A beautiful abyss, a poetry of hemp.

"Rassoul! Rassoul!"

Someone is shaking him. He sits up, slowly, opens his eyes, slowly; in his haze, he hears a teenage voice speaking to him.

"Hello. Razmodin sent me. He asked me to find you and take you to the Hotel Metropole. I've been looking for you everywhere . . ." Rassoul gazes at him from the depths of his dream ". . . I went to your house, and you weren't there. I went to the late Mohamaramollah's house . . ." Please, make him shut up! Rassoul isn't in the mood to listen to every moment of the search. The boy watches Rassoul light a cigarette and exclaims "It's a Marlboro!" in a voice full of envy. Rassoul offers him one. The boy hesitates, then takes it and sits down opposite Rassoul. ". . . Your fiancée told me she had lost you. I went back to your house, and the neighbor sent me here . . ." OK, OK! Rassoul gestures to show

86

that he has understood. Be quiet now; let him get his head together.

When he comes to his senses, Rassoul glances all around the room and sees only silent, motionless ghosts. "Your cousin nearly died!" Nearly died? Why? asks Rassoul with his eyes, frowning. "A rocket landed just behind the hotel. It caused a lot of damage." But Razmodin is safe?

Rassoul stands up suddenly and walks out of the smoking den, followed by the young lad. He runs—still limping—all the way to Razmodin's office, in the basement of the hotel. The door is open. His cousin is busy picking up papers that have scattered all over the floor.

Nothing serious, then.

I can leave.

Yes, leave! Or it will be the same words, the same reproaches, the same temper as this morning . . . Worse, in fact, because he will see that you've been smoking hash.

He is about to leave when Razmodin notices him. He stops gathering his things and rushes to the door. "Where are you going, Rassoul?" Rassoul freezes. "Come in!" Rassoul comes in. "Sit down!" commands Razmodin, pointing to a decrepit sofa. He is febrile, more so than this morning. Something is roiling inside him, troubling him, preventing him from speaking. Time passes. Time spent searching for the right words, words that can make bad news bearable. Rassoul senses this. He knows his cousin, knows his confusion and clumsiness in difficult situations. He waits for him to find the words.

"Rassoul, do you know Commandant Rostam?" Rassoul looks down, pretending to think, and keeps his head down as he shakes it, so as not to give anything away. Of course he knows him. He must be the man his mother mentioned in one of her letters, without giving his name—the one who wants to marry Donia. "He's come from Mazar, at your mother's request. He's upstairs now, waiting for you in the hotel restaurant," says Razmodin as he paces over to his desk. He returns to whisper the thing that is torturing him: "Cousin, there's bad news"; he waits, waits for Rassoul to stand up and cry: "What bad news?" But he doesn't, he just sits there quietly, motionless, avoiding Razmodin's eyes.

"Rassoul?" Rassoul looks up. "Your father . . ." He is dead—Rassoul knows that, but can't say it. And even if he could, he wouldn't; he'd nod his head, as he is doing now. That's all.

"He is . . . dead." Razmodin finally stutters out the word. Rassoul nods his head again to show that he already knows.

"You knew?" Rassoul mouths "yes" with his eyes on the ground. "You already knew?" repeats Razmodin, stunned. "How did you know? Who told you? When?"

Must I really find a pen and explain all this—how my mother told me a month ago, in a letter that she sent to this very hotel? Come on, Razmodin, you remember: it was you who brought me the letter. Don't act like an idiot!

No, Razmodin is not an idiot. He has understood

88

everything. The only reason he's stunned is that he can't understand why you didn't tell him. "But cousin, it was your father!" He grabs Rassoul by the arm, outraged. "They killed him! Did you know that?" Few people die a natural death these days, Razmodin. You know my opinion on the subject. So please, spare me this absurd astonishment, this fake surprise . . . Rather let us remain in this silence, laden as it is with your accusations and my despair.

Razmodin stares at him. Rassoul keeps his eyes on the ground, not in case he contradicts himself but so that his cousin won't see he's been smoking.

Hide as he may, Razmodin is beginning to suspect. That's why he leans over, checking Rassoul's dark, evasive eyes for the slightest sign, the slightest gleam to assure him of his cousin's state. He can't believe that Rassoul harbors such hatred toward his father.

No, it's not even hatred but something still more savage: indifference. And worse, not indifference at life itself, but at his father's death.

No, Rassoul cannot be this cruel, this inhuman. There must be something else going on.

Hash! That's what it is. Look at his eyes! So red, so lost, so dull . . .

"Have you been smoking again?"

Here we go!

Rassoul stands up and walks out. The door slams. Razmodin remains alone for a moment, bewildered. Then he comes to his senses and rushes into the corridor.

"Where are you going? Commandant Rostam is looking for you." Rassoul shrugs. What the hell does he care? "He's come all the way from Mazar-e-Sharif. He was a friend of your father's . . . He says he's going to take care of your mother and sister." He'd better come back another day. Rassoul is busy. "What's happening to you, cousin? You're not saying a word! Tell me what's going on!" Nothing, Razmodin, nothing! "Are you sick?" No, he shakes his head.

But you are sick, Rassoul, sick of yourself.

Razmodin follows him: "You've let yourself go again, not eating, not sleeping . . ." He takes a few notes and slips them into Rassoul's pocket. "Promise me you'll take care of yourself. See a doctor. Eat, rest, recover your strength. I'll come and check on you . . ."

Why such contempt for Razmodin, when he is such a kindly cousin?

Because I know why he's always taking such care of me. It is neither compassion nor friendship. It's because he too wants to marry my sister. That's why!

And?

Rassoul leaves the hotel, annoyed.

The street is still thick with smoke, and just as stifling. After a few steps Rassoul comes to a thoughtful standstill. "Who is this fucking Rostam?" He lights a cigarette, and glances across the road to the Ministry of Information and Culture. It is seething with armed men, Jano among them. He sees Rassoul and calls out, "Hey,

Rassoulovski!" Rassoul crosses the street. "So you've decided, have you? Follow me!" They enter the building, go down the stairs and along a dark, smoky basement corridor until they find Commandant Parwaiz talking to two bearded men around a large map of Kabul. Their voices are muffled by the roar of a generator. Jano walks up to Parwaiz to tell him that Rassoul has come.

"And how is my Dostoevsky scholar? Welcome. You look much younger than last night!" says Parwaiz with his disarming smile. Rassoul strokes his chin to indicate that it's because he has shaved off his beard. "The beard disgusted you?" Laugh. "And the voice?" Rassoul grimaces. "*Watandar,* why didn't you tell me last night that you were Razmodin's cousin? We met in prison. So . . . are you coming to join us?" Yes, he nods, glancing awkwardly at the two men. "They're with us," says Parwaiz in reassurance. After a brief silence, on account of his uncertainty about whether or not to say it, and how to say it, Rassoul picks up a pencil lying on the Kabul map and scribbles the name Commandant Rostam on one corner. Parwaiz reads it out and asks him, astonished: "You're going to join Commandant Rostam?" The two men turn and stare at Rassoul. This makes him even more nervous. One says: "Who doesn't know him!" and stares hard at Parwaiz, saying: "In fact, I wanted to talk to you about that. People are saying that you want to join forces with him."

"Yes, but . . ."

"Tell me it's just a rumor!"

"Sadly, it's true!"

"So that's why he's in Kabul! And you're up for it?"

"It's not for me to decide . . ."

"Think about what you're saying, Parwaiz: the day I find out that pig is with us is the day you'll see me across enemy lines."

"Commandant Morad, it is better to live in peace with him than . . ."

"In peace with one's enemy? Do you believe in peace between a wolf and a lamb?"

"What you are saying is true, but with our enemies we have a duty to make peace; with a friend, there's no need."

"But why? You're well aware that we can't stand each other! If you want to make peace with him then my place is no longer here with you. Goodbye!"

He takes his gun and strides out. Parwaiz and the other man rush after him. Rassoul remains there alone, distraught, staring at the map of Kabul laid out on the table, crumpled and full of holes.

At this point his sister's name reverberates inside him—"Donia!"

T HE CITY of Kabul is waiting for the wind. It waits for the wind as it waits for the rain to bring an end to the drought. Just five weeks ago, the wind would start blowing before the sun had even disappeared behind the mountains. It would raise all the dust that had covered the city and every inch of people's lives, and chase it away. That wind arose from none of the cardinal points. You could say it arose at the end of the earth, and to there it returned having whirled around the city to help it breathe, sleep, and dream once more . . . But it blows no longer. It lets everything stagnate: the sulphur of war, the smoke of terror, the embers of hatred. The fatty stench of burning clings to your skin, seeps into your bones. Better to smoke one of Nana Alia's cigarettes than to breathe this stifling air.

Rassoul lights up. No desire to go home, or to see Sophia. He is still wandering. Lost.

Perhaps he should find a doctor? With the money Razmodin gave him he could afford the consultation and the medicine, food, and something to smoke.

*   *   *

At the Malekazghar crossroads he sees a sign for a doctor's clinic, *"Specializing in ear, nose, and throat."* He walks in. The waiting room is full to bursting. Men and women with their families, some who seem to have spent the night there. People are eating, smoking, coughing, shouting, laughing . . .

At the entrance to the passage, a young man is handing out numbers. He shouts to Rassoul: "You have to arrive very early to get a number—around six in the morning." Seeing Rassoul's shocked face, he grumbles: "All Kabul comes here to be treated. Whether they have throat problems or piles! The hospital only takes the war wounded these days, and not all of them!"

Rassoul is about to leave when a woman approaches and says that if he needs to see the doctor urgently she will sell him her number for fifty afghanis. It is number ninety-six, tenth in the queue, "and you'll see, it goes quick! Fifty afghanis would buy milk and medicine for my child." Rassoul hesitates, then accepts and waits in the passage for his turn. As he waits he sees the woman sell three more numbers!

As luck would have it, the doctor is very old, and can barely see! This means that despite his hugely thick glasses he has trouble writing out the prescriptions. He tells his patients to speak up. Distraught, Rassoul scribbles "I've lost my voice" on a prescription form and holds it out to the doctor, who yells at him to read out what he's written, then suddenly understands. "Since

94

when?" Three days, he indicates on his fingers. "What caused it?" Silence. "A physical trauma?"

"..."

"Emotional?" Yes, nods Rassoul, after a moment's pause. "There's nothing I can give you for that," says the doctor maddeningly, drumming his fingers on piles of prewritten prescriptions for all kinds of complaints. "The only way to get your voice back is to relive the situation, the emotion. That'll be one hundred afghanis for the consultation, please." Then he calls out, "Next!" Before the next patient arrives, Rassoul pays with all the money he has left, and leaves the clinic in a rage to wander again through the unsettled city until night-fall. Then he goes home and sleeps. No nightmares.

THE NIGHTMARE is his life. Grace is but a dream. That's probably why he has no desire to open his eyes, to leave his bed, to greet the black sun, to smell the sulphur of war, to find his lost voice, or to think about the murder. He huddles deeper under his sheet. Eyes shut. Door shut. For a long time nothing drags him from this torpor. Not the flies flitting about his head; not the two rockets that land on Asmai; not the desperate footsteps of Razmodin as he climbs the stairs, waits behind the closed door, and goes away again; not the joyful cries of Yarmohamad's children playing in the courtyard . . . As long as the sun doesn't set, Rassoul doesn't rise.

But he does rise to the wicked woman in the sky-blue chador slipping slowly into his sleepy bed. Still veiled, she begins caressing Rassoul, who attempts to pull off her chador. She resists but Rassoul is stubborn. He tugs at the great expanse of fabric but it continues to slip through his fingers. The woman laughs. She holds out a casket. There is no jewelry inside, just a little ball, translucent and alive. "It's your Adam's apple," she says. "Do you want it?"

Rassoul throws the casket to the floor. He wants to see her face. He tries once more to pull off the chador; in vain. He finds himself enveloped too. He lacks the strength to rip the veil. He is suffocating.

He struggles.

Opens his eyes.

The sheet is what's suffocating him. The room is totally still, even the flies.

With a great sigh he sits up, clambers out of bed and leaves the house, to lose himself once more in the fog of the city.

He wanders until he finds himself at Joy Shir Square, where his pace is slowed by the smell of bread. He stops and waits for a charitable hand to give him some halwa. Among the crowd gathered in front of the bakery is a limping man using a too-big crutch. He looks like one of the two men who were with Sophia's father at the *saqi-khana*.

After buying his bread the man walks past Rassoul. There are poems engraved on the wooden crutch, as there were on the one belonging to Moharamollah. It's the same crutch!

So?

So he must have snatched it while his friend was dying in the rubble. He didn't have one, so he stole it to aid his escape. This crutch is too big for him. Dirty traitor!

Rassoul follows him—first with his eyes, then with his feet.

The man walks off down a busy lane with his crutch under one arm and the bread under the other. Halfway along, he stops to adjust the bread and notices Rassoul, who has stopped too. Disturbed by the intense eye contact the man sets off again and then takes a new lane, this one empty. Now he knows that Rassoul is following him. Frightened, he increases his pace. Rassoul does likewise, catching him up and blocking his way. The man clutches the bread under his arm, out of breath and terrified. "I've six mouths to feed and only one loaf of bread," he begs.

You see, Rassoul, the poor man has no idea who you are.

No, he doesn't. I shall introduce myself. I shall refresh his rotten memory.

Why won't he look at me!

The limping man looks at him, terrorized, waiting for a shout, a slap, a knife, a pistol . . . but there is nothing except Rassoul's raging, terrifying stare. "What do you want from me?" asks the man. "Who are you?" That is the question. Rassoul mouths the name MO-HA-RA-MOL-LAH. The man tries to follow his lips. "Mohammad? Oh, Kazeem's son? I thought you'd been killed. How come you're here?!" Now you're mixing up the dead and the living. Look properly. My name is RA-SSOUUUULLLL, relative of MO-HA-RA-MOL-LAH.

Rassoul grabs his arm, pulls him to the ground, and uses his finger to spell out Moharamollah's name on the dirt road. "Which Moharamollah?" Rassoul points at the crutch, hoping the man will associate it with the name. Hopeless. The man still doesn't understand what Rassoul wants from him. "You want my crutch?" No! "What do you want, then?" Rassoul points with his finger at the name on the ground. Panicking, the man reads it out again. "Are you Moharamollah? I don't know you." He stands up, and Rassoul follows. The man tries to step past him and continue home. Rassoul is quicker; he blocks the way, and stares into the man's terrified face.

Is it really him?

No doubt whatsoever. I'm going to help him remember all the times he spent with Moharamollah in the smoking den, and the day a rocket set fire to it. The only way he'll remember his betrayal is by re-experiencing the threat of death.

Rassoul snatches at the crutch, which the man grips in terror as he begs: "In the name of Allah!" Rassoul pretends not to hear. He secures the crutch and goes to strike the man with it. "Save me from this madman, Allah!" cries the man as he falls to the ground, clutching his bread. Rassoul crouches down and writes in the dirt: "I am a traitor." The man can barely make out the letters amid the pebbles and footprints. He forces himself to read. He is in such a state that he struggles to understand the meaning of the sentence, asking Rassoul: "You're a traitor?" No, you! gestures Rassoul as he points to the man's chest. "Me, a traitor! Why?" he exclaims. Rassoul brandishes the crutch above the horrified man as he stares at him in a fury. The man can barely breathe.

"You stole this from him," he writes next to the name Moharamollah. "I did not! That crutch is mine. I bought it. I swear to you . . ." But the crutch bashes his diseased leg, giving rise to a tortured scream. "Help!" Rassoul grabs him by the hair and holds his head to the ground so he will read aloud, "I am a traitor," but the man doesn't read, just yells even louder: "Help! Save me! Please help!" This time, the crutch lands on his head, quieting him. In tears, he begs: "My brother, are you not a Muslim? I've six children. Allah have mercy! I have no money. I swear to you, I have no money." Poor man. He doesn't know that if this was about money, his skull would have been cracked by now.

Let him go, Rassoul! He will never understand what you want from him, or why.

I want him to admit that he's a traitor. To shout it loud for everyone to hear.

The crutch is raised again and the man cries: "Don't strike! I give in. Don't strike!" The crutch is suspended in mid-air. "I betrayed . . . betrayed! Forgive me! Allah, I beg your forgiveness . . ." The crutch bashes his head once more; he screams in pain and fear. "Don't strike! I betrayed." Now he is shouting again, "I betrayed," louder, "I betrayed," louder still. May everyone hear you. Shout! "I am a traitor! A murderer!" No, you are not a murderer. YOU ARE A TRAITOR!

You belong in the Aliabad madhouse, Rassoul. How

can you expect this poor man to understand your obsessions? They are yours, not his. To him betrayal and murder are the same crime, of equal severity.

No. Of course he can tell them apart. He is from here, from this country where betrayal is worse than murder. You can kill, rape, steal . . . the important thing is not to betray. Not to betray Allah, your clan, your family, your country, your friend . . . Which is exactly what he's done!

No need for a pretext. Nothing justifies your savagery toward this man, nothing, unless you're trying to commit another murder in order to re-experience the same situation, the same trauma, the same emotion that made you mute. All this just to recover your voice?

Let the man live. Your voice or even the voice of a prophet is not worth a single life.

White as a sheet, Rassoul bashes the crutch against the wall so hard that it shatters. He sits down. The man is weeping.

Once he's got his breath back, Rassoul lights a cigarette and glances at the limping man, who is groaning as he attempts to stand. He lights another and gives it to him.

And he leaves.

Goes to the *saqi-khana.*

Kaka Sarwar and his crew aren't there but the den is packed. Everyone is staring at a madman with long hair and an unkempt beard. Each person gives him something: a glass of tea, a five hundred afghani note, a bullet. The madman takes the money first, then the bullet, which he puts into his mouth and swallows, and finally the glass of tea, which he gulps down in one. The man who gave the money turns to the others, stunned. "That's five bullets! Did you see? That's the fifth bullet he has swallowed."

The madman pays no mind to the general astonishment; he stands up, and with a hoarse cry—"Ya-*hoo*"—leaves the smoking den, a few men in his wake.

Rassoul exchanges two Marlboro for a long drag of hashish, and holds it in his lungs. He shuts his eyes. The world disappears, like the bullets into the man's mouth.

In the early hours he hears Kaka Sarwar's voice upstairs, in the *chai-khana*. He joins the crew, who offer to share their breakfast with him. Then he accompanies them back down to the *saqi-khana*.

By the time he leaves the smoking den he is high as a kite.

He is afraid to return home. He feels as if the ghosts from his nightmares have invaded his room: the woman in the sky-blue chador, Yarmohamad brandishing a knife, Razmodin and his moral lectures, and even Dostoevsky with his *Crime and Punishment* . . .

His unsteady feet take him toward Sophia's house.

What are you looking for from her?

I need her, and no one else. I need her to take me

into the purity of her tears, the candor of her smile, the space between her breaths . . . until I die in her innocence.

In other words you hope to absolve yourself with her naivety, her fragility. That's what it is! Leave her in peace. Don't drag her into your abyss.

He stops.

I will write it all down in her notebook, and give it to her. I will give her back her life.

He hurries. Limping. Stoned.

H E STRUGGLES to climb the stairs, make it to the door, and slip into his room. When he finally does, he is surprised to find his home tidy and clean. His clothes have been folded, his books piled up in one corner, and there is no broken glass on the floor.

Who has taken all this trouble? Yarmohamad's wife Rona, of course, as she used to before.

He walks to the window and glances at Yarmohamad's house. The courtyard is empty. No shadows behind the windows. An inner ecstasy takes hold of him, overcoming both his astonishment at his orderly room, and his tormented desire to write everything down for Sophia.

But what has made him so happy? His victory over Yarmohamad, who hasn't been able to prevent his wife from cleaning up after him?

What arrogance!

This vile, infantile joy shatters as his gaze falls on the infamous notebook, placed carefully on the window ledge. He falls on it. Did Rona open it, did she read his intimate poems and thoughts about Sophia? What about the final sentence, *"Today, I killed Nana Alia"*?

The notebook trembles in his hands. He opens it at the final page and reads, "*Today, I killed Nana Alia.*" He sits down on the mattress. Then, after great deliberation, he takes his pen and adds "*I killed her for you, Sophia.*"

For her? Why?

I will tell her, in writing. But first I want to write about her, her fragile innocence, all that I never knew how to describe in straightforward, precise words. "*Sophia, I have never kissed you. Do you know why?*" The words in his pen are suspended by the sound of footsteps ascending the stairs. Someone knocks at the door. A soft, feminine voice whispers: "Rassoul-*djan*, it's Rona." He leaps up to open the door. "Hello," she says shyly. She is carrying a tray, covered with a white napkin. He steps back to let her in and looks at her furtively, trying to gauge how she will react to the notebook in his hand. "Rassoul-*djan*, I have come to beg forgiveness for Yarmohamad. He is not in his right mind these days. He's a bundle of nerves. He's afraid . . . You know him. And what's more, he has no work. He is just worried . . ." She holds out the tray: "Look, here is *kishmish-panir*, homemade raw cheese, the kind you like, and raisins."

Embarrassed, Rassoul takes the tray and thanks her with a vague gesture, as if to say that she mustn't worry, it's all over with now. Then, to express his gratitude for the cleaning, he bows low and gestures with the hand holding the notebook at the corner where all his books are neatly stacked. "I did it like I used to. Back when . . ."

He is no longer listening. Reassured that there is no suspicion or anxiety in her gaze, he is fascinated, as usual, by her plump shining lips and hazel, almond-shaped eyes. She is aware of her allure—always has been—and she teases him, biting the edge of her veil to hide her lips. That turns him on even more. Rassoul is sure that the real reason Yarmohamad has it in for him is his soft spot for Rona. Surely he suspects the attraction.

"Right, I'm off . . ." She makes up her mind to leave. Rassoul follows, embarrassed not to have heard what she said from behind her veil. He stands in the doorway, watching her until she disappears into the darkness of her own front door. He looks for Yarmohamad behind the windows. No sign. He must have gone out; that's why Rona dared to visit.

If Rassoul weren't so distracted, if he didn't have so many worries, if Sophia's notebook weren't in his hand, he would lie down on his mattress and surrender to his fantasies. His hand would slip into his trousers to stroke himself, and as he did so he would imagine Rona in two or three different scenes. Today, he would go for the one where she's completely naked, sitting on her daughters' swing, head tilted slightly back, a sly smile on her lips. She is staring straight into Rassoul's eyes. Legs spread, swing ropes curled around her arms, hands on her pubis, touching herself . . . But this just isn't the time. He'd have to be really sick—obsessed, an escapee from the Aliabad loony bin—to think of that now!

Put down the tray, close the door, and get back to your writing.

He opens the notebook.

Sophia, I have never kissed you. Do you know why? What next? *Because I would have needed such strength to kiss your innocence . . .* What the hell is that? Why can't your thoughts be clearer, your words more direct? Kiss your innocence! What does that mean? If you write that she'll tease you, saying: "Smash my innocence! Kiss me! And I'll give you strength."

Drained, Rassoul closes the notebook, chucks it on top of the books and flops on his bed. He shuts his eyes to find in the silence and darkness the words that he seeks. But footsteps on the stairs drag him back out of bed. Heavy footsteps, this time. "Rassoul! It's Razmodin." He is not alone, someone is whispering. Rassoul doesn't move. "Rassoul?" repeats Razmodin, knocking at the door. After a short pause, he calls out to Yarmohamad's daughters. "Hello, girls! Has Rassoul left?"

"No, he's in his room. Perhaps he's sleeping," they reply together. Go to hell! bellows Rassoul to himself. He stands up.

"Rassoul!" calls Razmodin again, rattling the door, which is locked from the inside. He knocks harder. Give me a moment, mutters Rassoul silently. He opens the door.

"Ah, there you are, finally! We've been looking for you for two days," exclaims Razmodin as he enters; behind him is a thin little man, wearing a white turban. "Rassoul, Commandant Rostam has been kind enough to come and visit you and . . ." The Commandant walks toward Rassoul, "My dear Rassoul," and embraces him, "how good to meet you at last!" Rassoul steps back, cold and unwelcoming. Rostam remains on the threshold, waiting to be invited in. Razmodin takes the initiative, rushing into the room and gesturing a welcome. Rostam enters and launches into a ceremonious speech: "My dear Rassoul, I have come on behalf of your venerable mother. I don't know where to begin. I carry two pieces of news from your family. One, sadly, unfavorable and most sad; the other good and full of hope. I must tell you, with great sorrow, that your father, who was a good and pure Muslim, has bravely given up his soul to Allah the Merciful. He died a martyr. I offer you all my condolences. May he dwell in heaven. And I pray to Allah the Merciful to accord the family that survives him much fortitude, and a long and prosperous life . . ." He lifts his hands to pray, "*Ina-ellahe wa ina-ellaïhe radi´oun.*" After this he is quiet, waiting for Rassoul to speak. Rassoul stares at him impassively. More embarrassed than shocked, Rostam glances discreetly at Razmodin and then, without waiting to be asked, takes off his shoes and sits on the mattress. Razmodin follows suit. The two of them stare at Rassoul, who sits down impassively a little way off.

Silence.

A gloomy silence that Rostam tries to break by offering a cigarette to Rassoul—who refuses—and then to Razmodin; after that he continues with his speech: "Of course, your dear mother told me that she had informed you of these regrettable events by post . . . but I can see that her letter has not reached you . . ." The commandant is made even more uncomfortable by Rassoul nodding his head and scrunching his eyebrows to convey that he certainly did receive the letter. Rostam looks on helplessly as Rassoul starts rummaging through his books to find his mother's letter and wave it under the dazed eyes of his guests; then he returns to his spot and nonchalantly picks up a plastic swatter to chase away the flies swarming around the tray of *kishmish-panir*.

"You did receive it, then?" asks the commandant.

Yes.

"But . . . your respected mother believes you are not aware of your father's martyrdom! Ever since she sent you that letter she has been waiting for you to arrive."

Rassoul stares reproachfully at Razmodin, who keeps his eyes down, fixed on the tips of his nails as he waits fearfully for his cousin to say: "My father had little importance to me, alive or dead." It seems Razmodin has not discussed it with Rostam. But why not? He should have!

Rassoul brings down the swatter on a fly that had landed on the floor in front of him, and flicks the corpse toward the door. Rostam gets the message; he is furious, and can barely contain himself: "You know quite well that for a young Afghan Muslim, duty toward one's parents is the most important of all values. The blood of a father is priceless. We were all expecting you to swear to avenge him." He is interrupted by the swatter coming down on another fly. He turns toward Razmodin, exasperated: "Do you know how greatly this young man's mother and sister will suffer if they hear how he is behaving toward them and the late Ibrahim?" Razmodin nods, while imagining what Rassoul must be thinking: "No, they are probably relieved at my father's death."

Rostam is more and more frustrated by Rassoul's silence. He takes a long drag on his cigarette and waits. In vain. He becomes impatient. "Say something, in the name of Allah!" Rassoul lets go of the swatter and stares at him imperiously for a long moment. Razmodin knows exactly what is seething inside Rassoul, but can't understand why his cousin remains silent. Out of respect? That would be most unlike him. He must be weighing his words—the better to insult, as usual, all those who in the name of tradition, honor, and religion encourage people to kill each other, avenge themselves, and thus feed the ongoing war . . . "Do you know who killed your father?" Rassoul shrugs; he doesn't care. "It was a thief, a crook, and he killed him for money . . . for money!" So it was someone who was hungry. There's no point taking revenge on a starving individual. As a communist, my father used to say he fought for justice on behalf of the hungry; he killed the rich to save the poor, didn't he? His soul must be rejoicing to see a few starving people feeding their bellies on his resources!

Razmodin is terrified by the mere thought of what is churning around in Rassoul's mind. And yet he's astonished, no, not astonished, relieved, to see him remaining quiet. Better take advantage. So he turns to Rostam to apologize on Rassoul's behalf: "My cousin hasn't been well these past few days . . . ," but is interrupted by Rassoul suddenly standing up, putting Rostam's shoes outside the door, and signaling him to leave.

Rostam is beside himself; he leaps to his feet, yelling: "What a *beadab* boy! So ungrateful!" Then he says to Razmodin: "If it weren't for respect for his mother and sister, I'd have kicked his guts in right there and then!" He spits on the floor at Rassoul's feet. But before Rassoul can react, Razmodin maneuvers Rostam out of the door.

Rassoul closes it behind them and stands in the middle of his room, listening to his cousin running after the commandant: "Please don't be angry, and don't take it to heart. He is sick, I promise. He's been acting strange ever since his father died. All month people have been complaining about him . . ." As they disappear down the lane, his voice fades away.

Emptied of his rage, Rassoul sits down with a triumphant smile. He picks up the swatter and looks around for another victim. No sooner does a fly land on his mattress than it is destroyed and flicked over to the door.

Now that he is calm, he picks up his mother's letter and reads it from beginning to end. Thank God she doesn't have fancy handwriting or a way of stretching things out to ten pages like Raskolnikov's mother! Her letter is short, badly written, and almost illegible.

He rereads the sentences concerning his sister Donia. *There is a rich and powerful man asking for your sister's hand . . .* But who? Why does his mother not mention his name? *Rich and powerful* must mean that he is not unknown. It must be someone controversial, with a bad reputation. That's why his mother doesn't want him to know who she is talking about.

His eyes stray over the letter, trying to avoid the words he doesn't want to read. But here they are, more legible than the rest: "*Donia is in agreement. But first she wants your approval. You are now the man of the house . . .*" He folds the letter. *The man of the house.* The first time he read it, that sentence filled him with pride—*the man of the house*—but now he sees that it conceals another, almost offensive, message. Each word has a new color, a new sound. They are no longer naïve and innocent. They emanate irony, reproach, and hidden meanings.

The man of the house!

No, your mother could never write a letter like that. It is you who has taken it badly. Read it again another day, and you'll see that it contains nothing but wisdom and kindness.

He folds the letter to slip it into a book. But not just any book. One of the volumes of *Crime and Punishment*, of course! And worse still: at the very page where Raskolnikov reads his mother's letter.

This is too much, Rassoul!

He hasn't yet put the book back in its place when the door bursts open and Razmodin's voice fills the room: "Are you on a death mission, or what? Do you want to be hit by a stray bullet? What the hell do you want? You really must be sick." Rassoul looks at him, wondering whether to give him his mother's letter. "Why did you behave like such an idiot? Do you know that he's taken my aunt and Donia under his own roof, so as not to leave them alone? He came all this way to reassure you and give you money. Here!" He takes a wad of notes from his pocket and flings it onto the mattress. "Not only did you not thank him, you didn't even speak to him! Why?" Shaken, Rassoul opens the book, takes out the letter and gives it to Razmodin. Read! And he reads it. Each word drains him, drives his head deeper into his shoulders, makes his hand tremble. Now let him understand what this cash is all about! That's right, this generosity and kindness aren't to please Rassoul. Rostam intends to buy Donia with this money. Donia, your cousin. The woman you love and want to marry. "Was that the 'good news' the son of a bitch wanted to tell you, then?" asks Razmodin hopelessly. That's why Rassoul treated him so rudely— to stop him announcing his news in front of you. "Donia!" exclaims Razmodin. He seizes Rassoul by the shoulders, and asks him dully: "But . . . but why didn't you tell me?" Rassoul shakes himself free. "If you had told me, I would have gone to Mazar, and taken you with me . . ." Well, go there now, and leave Rassoul in peace. "I'm taking you with me." Rassoul can't go anywhere anymore. Go, Razmodin, and bring his mother and Donia back to Kabul!

Razmodin springs to his feet, on fire: "We'll go and get them . . ." But Rassoul's despairing gaze crushes his enthusiasm and brings him back to his senses: "No, things are becoming very dangerous, here. We'll all go to Tajikistan." Rassoul shakes his head. "You're right, that's under their control, too"—he is weary now—"so where? Find a solution, damn it!" Do what you want, but leave Rassoul in peace. In peace!

Torn between his rage at Rassoul's incomprehensible silence and his anxiety at the threat posed by Rostam, Razmodin stands dejected for a moment. Then suddenly he leaves, slamming the door. His furious steps can be heard charging down the stairs, hammering through the courtyard, and at last disappearing into the dust of nightfall.

Exhausted, Rassoul shuts his eyes, but cannot sleep.

Night falls, dark.
It invades the room.

And when the chorus of calls to prayer seizes the city from its sleep, Rassoul painfully opens his eyes. His head is spinning. He sits up and leans against the wall, his legs bent to his chest.

He is trembling. Trembling with rage, fear, cowardice . . . with everything.

Everything joins together in his chest.

Swells up and bursts out of his throat, silently.

He weeps.

H E SLEEPS.

Suddenly, he is jolted awake by the terrifying sound of an explosion. Soaked in sweat, he scrambles to a sitting position and looks wildly out of the window. It is still night, still dark. The black smoke forbids the moon from slipping inside, into peoples' dreams.

Rassoul lights the candle that Rona has left within his reach. He drags himself to the clay jug. Not a drop of water.

Returning to bed, he suddenly sees the bundle of notes that Rostam left in Razmodin's care. A fly has landed on it. The bundle is just like the one Nana Alia grasped so firmly in her stiff, fleshy hand. Or at least it reminds him of that. All cash looks the same.

Pick it up!

After a long hesitation he snatches it, as if hoping to capture the fly as well. But it escapes back to its friends on the white napkin draped over the raw cheese and raisins.

He stares at the money for a long time, before flinging it into a corner of the room. Out of fear, or revulsion.

He smokes.

He thinks.

He thinks that maybe this cash is not as dirty as the stuff that belonged to Nana Alia after all. Or as dangerous. So why such disgust? "Egotism!" Razmodin would say. "You really are eaten up by egotism, Rassoul. An egotism based on nothing, an absurd egotism."

Yes, I admit to this baseless egotism. May the world know: I prefer egotism to pride. To be proud is to be proud of *something*, and therefore to depend on that thing. Whereas egotism is something deep, internal, personal, independent, with no external reference point. Pride relates to honor; egotism to dignity.

Words again, pretty words. Despite everything you've been through and are going through, you still can't come to terms with the fact that you need this money. That's nearly fifty thousand afghanis—enough to save your mother, your sister, and your fiancée. Letting your family be destroyed: Now wouldn't that be an affront to this egotism, this dignity?

Rassoul, exasperated, takes a long drag on his cigarette, and on the exhale blows out the candle. He lies down and waits in the darkness. Waits for the dawn to rise so he can visit his cousin, and give him back the money.

No, it is not with this money that I will save my family.

If you say so. But with what, then?

He tosses and turns; with his nail he scrapes a chunk of peeling paint from the wall. He did this as a boy, licking the remains of the foul-smelling paint from his fingertips; licking it in order to make himself throw up, and to stop himself from sleeping.

He does not throw up.

He falls asleep.

By dawn he is at the Hotel Metropole. The neighborhood has been cordoned off and is protected by two tanks, a few armed jeeps, and several UN vehicles. Rassoul strides purposefully up to the hotel. He is stopped by two armed men. He moves his lips to form the name Razmodin.

"What?"

Suddenly, there is a great commotion. Men pass by carrying the body of a "martyr" and yelling: "Allah-o Akbar! Avenge our *shahids*!" The two guards abandon Rassoul to join the procession. He walks into the hotel. The lobby is packed with armed men and journalists, all waiting for something to happen. What? No one seems to know. Everyone is on edge. Rassoul heads for the stairs to Razmodin's office, but is forced to melt into a corner when he sees Commandant Rostam appear at the far end of the corridor flanked by the two men Rassoul met in Parwaiz's office—the ones who swore lifelong hatred for the commandant from Mazar. They look in good spirits despite the tense atmosphere in the hotel, and seem to be on the same side . . .

Rassoul slips into Razmodin's office. He is not there.

He must have gone to Mazar, to fetch Donia. Now there's a real man. Doing what needs to be done. Good.

Yes, good, because it lets you off the hook.

I've had enough. Think of me as a coward. A good-for-nothing. I am just a failed son, failed friend, failed enemy, failed student, failed fiancé, failed murderer . . . and that is all I am. Leave me to inebriate myself, to take a trip into the poetic abyss of hemp.

And he knocks on the door of the *saqi-khana*. "Who's there?" asks Hakim, the owner, as he peers through the gaps in the door. "Rassoul?" Yes. "But which one? The saint or the hash-head?" calls Kaka Sarwar. Hakim opens the door laughing, and pulls Rassoul inside. As always, the curls of smoke make everything look blurred and hazy, as in a dream.

Hakim shuts the door and shows Rassoul to a place in the circle of smokers, next to a young man in a trancelike state. "Move up, Jalal, make some space."

Another young man sitting next to Jalal moves instead, saying: "Don't spoil his high. Jalal is as high as a kite. If he moves, he'll come down. Sit here, my friend, next to Mustapha. That's a good spot for you." Once Rassoul has sat down, Mustapha hands him the chillum. "Here, for you, the new arrival." Rassoul first breathes out the sulphurous air of the city, then draws in as much hashish as his lungs will hold.

"Our friend Jalal was born on opium. He was big, apparently. It was only the opium that allowed his

mother to get him out. So he was born high on opium
... the lucky thing!" As he breathes out the smoke
Rassoul glances at Jalal, who looks up and murmurs:
"The war hasn't started yet, has it?" Mustapha asks in
a whisper: "What are they saying outside—another coup
d'état?" Rassoul shrugs his shoulders to indicate that
he has no idea, and takes another lungful.

"He doesn't know either, Kaka Sarwar!" says
Mustapha, pointing at Rassoul. "So he can't be Rassoul
the Sacred Messenger."

Kaka Sarwar shakes his head. "Not knowing anything
about anything is the essence of wisdom. This young
man has understood life. He knows everything, but
knows nothing about it."

Another head looms out of the smoke: "It's been
years now that we've known nothing about anything,
and the world has known nothing about us. Is that
wisdom, then?"

"It's not the same thing."

"Then I no longer understand what you're saying,
Kaka Sarwar."

"Listen, when you say that you don't know anything,
that's the beginning of wisdom. And when you say that
you don't know anything about anything, then you have
attained absolute wisdom. Do you know anything about
this war?"

"No."

"Very good. You know that you don't know. That's
a great start! And once you understand the why of this

war, you will wish that you didn't know. Come on, pass me the chillum!" He smokes, then continues: "A holy man among holy men, by the name of Attar, used to say that in the penultimate valley of wisdom—which he called Wadi Hayrat—the traveler would be stupefied, and become lost. He would forget everything, even himself." He closes his eyes and recites a poem: *"If he is asked: 'Are you, or are you not? Have you or have you not the feeling of existence? Are you in the middle or on the border? Are you mortal or immortal?' he will reply with certainty: 'I know nothing, I understand nothing, I am unaware of myself. I am in love, but with whom I do not know. My heart is at the same time both full and empty of love.'"*

"So, are we in this valley?" asks Hakim, making the smokers laugh.

"If, instead of asking stupid questions, you manage to stupefy us with your hashish, then YES!" says Kaka Sarwar, taking a long drag on the chillum and passing it to Jalal, who has come back to life: "So the war hasn't started."

"It's already finished. Smoke, smoke and chill out!" reassures Mustapha. Then, to Rassoul: "He's scared of the war, you see. He's afraid of blood and bullets and rockets. That's why he'd rather kill himself smoking than die in the war. We've been staggering from one *saqi-khana* to the next for four days now."

The chillum has gone out. Jalal looks up, completely wasted: "Is it finished?"

"The war? Yes."

"No, the hash . . ."

Hakim moves forward to pass him another pipe. "Do you have the money?"

"Money . . . Mustapha, have you . . . ?"

"No, dear Jalal. Our pockets are as dry as our arses."

Rassoul stands up unsteadily, pulls a 500-afghani note from his pocket, and gives it to Jalal. Everyone stares at him in shock and admiration. He takes out another 500 and gives it to Hakim to buy everyone a kebab.

They all thank him loudly. He leaves the smoking den feeling proud and light. Lighter than air. What joy! From now on he's going to live on Rostam's money as he could have lived on Nana Alia's. In dignity and happiness.

Now I'm going to find Sophia. I'm going to take her in my arms. We'll be married. I will take her—take both our families—far away, far beyond this realm of terror.

He runs.

A rocket shakes the earth under his feet.

He runs.

Nothing holds him back. Not gunshot, not traffic, not the pain in his ankle.

Nothing affects him. Not cries, not tears, not the calls for help.

He only stops when he reaches Sophia's house. He pauses a moment to regain his breath, then knocks on the gate.

After a long silence it opens. Dawoud. Hey, he's not on the roof! "The pigeons don't fly at this time of day." Dawoud closes the gate behind them and follows Rassoul in a state of great excitement. "My pigeon came back. As soon as you left, it came back. I think it flew a long way." He laughs nervously. "I've already swapped it for . . ." Happy and proud, he heads to the corner of the courtyard, takes something from under the pigeon cage, and brings it to Rassoul. "Look, this is what I swapped it for . . ." A Colt. "In good condition!" says Dawoud. Rassoul checks the magazine; it is loaded. "I got it for you . . ." For him? What is he supposed to do with it? "Everybody has one, except you! If you have one, you won't die. Hide it so that my mother doesn't see it." Dawoud takes it from him anxiously, and conceals it under his shirt. "Your cousin came by. He was looking for you. He said he was going to Mazar." Rassoul walks down the passage and sees a light on in the kitchen. He walks in and greets Sophia's mother. "How are you, my son? Razmodin came by; he told us about your father. May God rest his soul and may he dwell in Heaven. How are your mother and sister?" She avoids Rassoul's gaze. "What a journey ahead, for your poor mother!" For mourning, there is silence.

And Sophia? Where is she?

Rassoul peers out into the passage. No sound, no sign of her. "I asked Nazigol for some money, telling myself that for once my children were going to eat their fill," she says, as if justifying something. But what? She bends over her stove, looking into the pots as if they might contain her words. After a long pause, she says: "Sophia has gone to Nana Alia's house." Her voice is curt, too curt. "Nazigol came over to find her. She's all alone. Her mother has disappeared off somewhere. There's lots to do, and Sophia won't be back till late." But Rassoul asked her to never go back there. And she has. In other words, his instructions no longer mean anything to her. That's it, then. He turns to leave, but Sophia's mother stops him without turning around: "Rassoul . . ." A pause that presages no good. "I've . . . I've one or two things to say to you." This is it. Rassoul is going to hear what he has been dreading she will say. "But I don't know how to say them." She wipes her nose on a corner of her headscarf. "Don't take this badly. I know that we understand each other . . ." Yes, Rassoul understands you perfectly. He's been waiting awhile now to hear you say what's on your mind. Tell him everything. "Until when are we going to wait for you? Especially now that your life has changed. Your mother and sister need you, even more than we do. You must go and take care of them." Rassoul feels as if his body is emptying. Emptying of blood, hope, life. He is just a wisp of straw, futile, dry, and tiny, to be tossed on the ground, or whisked away by the slightest breeze. He leans on the wall so as not to collapse under the feet of Sophia's mother, who continues: "We have to think of ourselves now; we can't just keep waiting for you forever. You have nothing anymore. No work. No money. Until when? Let us take ourselves in hand, and find a solution." But he loves Sophia. "Go home to your mother, Rassoul! We will manage. Don't worry." But he loves Sophia.

Yes, she knows that. And that's why she is quiet, now, holding back her words and expressing her thoughts only with a gaze full of pity and sadness for Rassoul. He looks down. After a long moment, he walks out of the kitchen and down the passage. In a corner of the courtyard he sees Dawoud working on a pigeon's wounded wing by the light of an oil lamp. Rassoul takes out the bundle of notes and gives it to Dawoud. "What's this?" Money for his Colt. Dawoud is delighted. He takes the money and holds out the pistol. "All this money is for me?" Yes. "All of it?" All of it. "How many pigeons can I buy with this?" Rassoul leaves him to his calculations, disappearing down the dusty streets of Dehafghanan like a shadow in the darkness, uncertain and empty.

Yes, empty. Empty of all substance.

No, Rassoul, you are not empty. You are simply free. Free of all constraint, all responsibility. Free because Sophia no longer needs you. And neither do your mother and sister.

Yes, this is emptiness: when nobody needs me, when I have nothing left to give. When whether I live or die changes nothing for them.

Exactly. Without you, the world will not be empty, but emptied of you. That's all.

I don't want to drag Sophia into this emptiness.

So, leave her!

I'm going to leave her. But first I've got to tell her that Nana Alia is no longer alive, that I killed her with my own hands.

She'll find that out sooner or later. This evening she's with Nazigol, who is offering the "hospitality" her mother used to provide. Amer Salam and his guests are bound to be there. What are you going to do?

Rassoul stops.

Inside, a sob he doesn't know how to dissolve. He rummages in his pocket for a cigarette, knocking the pistol with his hand. A hand that is trembling. Oozing tears. Weeping for his death.

A BODY crashes to the floor. Rassoul opens his eyes. Through the veil of smoke he can just make out Jalal. He drags himself over and gives the young man a shake. Hopeless; he is lying on the floor, a line of spittle dribbling from his mouth. "That's a happy man," murmurs Kaka Sarwar, curled up with his eyes closed. "He's not moving," says a young man next to Rassoul. Kaka Sarwar opens one eye, glances at Jalal and repeats: "That's a happy man. Born high, dying high."

"What can we do for him?"

"Nothing," whispers Mustapha, stoned, in another corner of the *saqi-khana*, his hands huddled under his armpits.

"He wants to die. Now that our lives depend on others, allow us the right to die," says Kaka Sarwar, closing his eyes again and droning into his beard: "*We come and go, but for the gain, where is it? / And spin life's woof, but for the warp, where is it? / And many a righteous man has burned to dust / In heaven's blue rondure, but their smoke, where is it?*"

Rassoul backs away, to sit against the wall and stare at Jalal, waiting to witness the arrival of another death.

127

A peaceful, gentle death. It will remove Jalal from this hell. Stop him dying from a stray bullet, or the blade of an ax. A death without suffering. And there will be no one to accuse, to condemn, or to execute. There will be neither crime nor punishment.

Rassoul takes out a cigarette and lights it, then stands up and leaves the smoking den to return to his fly-ridden room. He walks over to the bed, crushes his cigarette on the wall and lies down. Something in his pocket is bothering him. The gun. He rests it on his chest. What is to be done? He asks himself. What is to be done? he repeats in the silence of his throat, then tries to shout the question in the hope that the words will ring out from his lips, into this room, at the foot of the mountain, above the city . . . But there is no sound at all, no response.

What is to be done; it must be said without a question mark. It is not a question, but a thought. No, it's not even a thought, it's a state of being. Yes, that's right, a state of dullness, a state in which questions astound rather than challenge, ring out rather than inquire.

What is to be done.

I have already experienced this state, already seen it, I've even seen it in the eyes of a donkey.

It was autumn, and I was eleven years old.

As every year at that season, my father took me hunting near Jalalabad, where my grandparents had a great *qal'a* or clay fortress. The country hadn't yet been invaded by the Russians, the war hadn't yet started, and my father still got on well with his anti-communist in-laws.

As usual, we had a donkey to carry our hunting equipment and to guide us through the featureless deserts and valleys. After a long journey, we came to an enormous reed field surrounding a large lake. The perfect place for hunting migrant birds. We tied the donkey to a lone, dead tree not far from the field.

At the lakeside, we built a makeshift shelter in which we could wait for the birds. It was still early. While we waited, my father drifted off to sleep.

The gentle wind caressed the reeds, making them whistle a lovely, peaceful, sleep-inducing tune. I gradually dozed off, and slept for a long time. By the time I opened my eyes, the dusk had already enveloped the field in a strange, sad, and disturbing fog.

My father was very excited and kept looking up at the sky, saying that the migrant birds wouldn't be long now. He checked his shotgun several times.

The minutes went by, night was falling, but there was no sound, and no sign from the sky.

Silence.

Emptiness.

Suddenly, the donkey's braying invaded the field; quiet to start with, then louder and louder, frightened and frightening.

My father told me to go and see what was happening. I hesitated; I was scared. He shouted at me to go and quiet the beast or else the birds would never land. I went, the blood frozen in my veins. At the edge of the field I was horrified to see two wolves snarling and prowling around the donkey, preparing to attack. The trapped animal could do nothing but bray.

I panicked and ran to tell my father. He rushed furiously through the reeds with his gun. At first he tried to scare away the wolves by pelting them with stones, but they turned on us. Their gleaming eyes made them look terrifying. Even more afraid than before, I hid behind my father who cocked his gun and pointed it at the wolves. At the very moment they were about to attack a shot rang out and one of the wolves fell to the floor crying. The other beast stopped, and as my father took aim backed away and ran off.

The donkey was still braying.

We had to get out of there as fast as possible, before the whole pack arrived. My father went back into the reeds to get our things while I rushed over to calm the donkey by stroking it and loosening its halter. It quieted eventually.

As he harnessed the donkey my father kept glancing up, grumbling and cursing at the filthy fucking sky.

We left.

Night was falling, the moon was shining, the donkey led the way and we followed. From time to time my father lit up the path with his torch. We climbed a hill. At the top, the donkey came to a standstill. My father hit it on the rump, but it refused to go any further. It was looking fearfully at the track. My father hit it again, harder this time, and it started moving slowly forward. I was afraid that we would get lost, but my father assured me that the donkey knew the path and that the village couldn't be far away, perhaps another hour's walk.

We walked down the hill, through another field, and up another hill. As we reached the top, the donkey once again came to a standstill. My father's beatings forced it to proceed down the slope against its will.

At the foot of that hill, another huge field opened up in front of us, with a single tree in the middle. The donkey headed straight for the tree. As we approached, we could just make out in the twilight the corpse of an animal, with another beast standing watch. My father switched on his torch. It was the body of a wolf. The second wolf looked up. We were rooted to the spot, appalled. My father loaded his gun. The donkey was fearlessly approaching the wolves. The live one walked up to it, growling. As soon as my father took aim, it ran away.

The donkey walked past the dead wolf and stopped under the tree. My father's torch lit up the body of the animal, then the tree, and finally the surrounding area. Both of us were first surprised and then horrified to find ourselves back in the same place where my father had killed the wolf. My voice shaking, I asked my father why the donkey had brought us back to the same place. He had no idea. He rushed wildly over to the donkey, and walloped it on the back to make it move. But the donkey stood quite still. Unbelievable. My father picked up the stick and passed me the rope, telling me to pull. In vain—the beast had decided to go no further. I could see that in its dull, tired eyes. I stroked and begged, to no avail. My father was becoming more and more furious. He gave me the stick, grabbed the rope, and shouted at me to hit the donkey on the back and head.

But my heart wasn't in it. My half-hearted blows annoyed my father, who shouted and cursed at me. His shouts and the howling of the wolves rang out together across the plain.

On the verge of tears, I started hitting the donkey in impotent fury. To no effect. Discouraged and exhausted, I gave up and burst into tears. My father let go of the donkey's rope and whacked it on the head with the butt of his gun. It fell down and wouldn't get up. Everything seemed pointless: my tears, the cries of the wolves as they circled closer and closer, my father's stormy orders as he took up the stick to stab its point into the donkey's skin, swearing that if it didn't move he would put the barrel of the gun up its rear end and shoot. But the donkey remained impassive and unchanging, lying on the ground. My father was beside himself. He lifted his gun to take aim at the donkey; it stared at him without moving.

I stopped sobbing. The silence was broken only by the howling of the wolves. The gun trembled in my father's hand. I closed my eyes, and all I heard was a single shot, followed by the panic-stricken screeching of birds as they flew over the reed field. There was blood streaming from the beast's forehead. Its resigned eyes opened for a moment and closed again gently, as if relieved. Then absolute silence. No bird noise, nothing from the wolves. Everything seemed frozen against the black backdrop of the night.

Once his rage had subsided and he had come back to his senses my father quickly reloaded his gun; then, with our belongings on his back, he started walking, shouting to me: "Rassoul! Come on, move! Rassoul?"

Rassoul is haunted by this strange story, which he has titled "Nayestan"—the reed field. It lives in him, silently and religiously. His father, too, used to tell the story over and over again, wherever he was, at any time, to anyone. Each time, he would ask Rassoul to fill in the details he had forgotten. This was to establish him as a witness to the incredible adventure—but Rassoul didn't like joining in, and would leave as soon as his father started the story. Not that he'd had enough of it. No. It was just that he would have liked the story to remain a secret between him and his father. Why? He had no idea. And he still doesn't know. But he often tells himself the story, from beginning to end. And each time he adds something and leaves something else out. From time to time, he lingers on a particular moment or image that is particularly pertinent to his current state of mind. That is why he has never wanted to write the story down, to fix it on paper. If he wrote it down, it would be flawless, featureless, dead. In any case, he is no longer able to tell what his father has added and what he himself has introduced; what is true and what is made up; what belongs to memory and what to his dreams . . . But it doesn't matter. What is curious right now is that he keeps thinking about the look in the donkey's eyes. What was hidden behind that dumb gaze?

Everything. That lost, innocent, incredulous gaze cried out to him: "But why am I lost? Why can't I find my way? Where is the path? Is this not the path I've always taken? What's going on? Why can't I recognize where I am? Why is this road so foreign to me? Is it because it's night-time? Or because I'm afraid? Tired? Uncertain?" From a lack of response, these questions turned into a kind of stupor. To hell with the reasons why. The donkey was there, lost. And it knew that it would never find its way again. So all it could do was groan: "What is to be done," with no question mark.

What is to be done. Rassoul sits up. The pistol slips from his sweat-drenched chest. His heart is beating madly, as if about to explode, to burst from his chest and land next to the weapon.

He grabs the pistol with a trembling hand and points it at the top of his nose, just between his eyes. He presses the trigger. It isn't loaded, he knows that; he just wants to practice, to find out how easy it is to shoot himself in the head.

It is easy, very easy in fact. All he has to do is close his eyes.

He closes his eyes.

To no longer think. No longer think about anything. Or anyone. Not even his enemy, his hatred, his failure.

He is no longer thinking about those things.

Focus on the pistol. His soul is the bullet; his body, the trigger. The only thing remaining is the action, as simple as a game. A game with no winners or losers, no opponents. You just have to believe in the game, your game. And think only of the action. Nothing else. Not the realness of the game, nor its futility. The only thing that matters is to execute it well, following the rules. And not to cheat.

Now, he must load the bullet, and put the pistol back between his eyes.

The pistol is heavy.

Or his hand is weakening.

He is thirsty.

You mustn't think about water, either. Just tell yourself it's a game, and that when the game is over, you can stand up and drink some water.

You close your eyes.

And you shoot.

135

ARE YOU dying, then?

Yes, I'm dying. I'm dying from a hole between the eyes from which a stream of blood is spurting, running onto the mattress, then the kilim, and ending up in a hollow of the floor, where it forms a red pool. The shot rings out in the room, the courtyard, the city. It wakes Yarmohamad. He thinks that someone has fired a shot in the street, outside his house. He turns over in bed. Rona is worried and insists that he check the shot wasn't fired inside the complex, at me. Yarmohamad doesn't give a damn. "Good riddance," he mutters, huddling deeper under the sheet.

At dawn, after prayers, he will come to my room and stand silently at the door.

Why would he come?

Yes, why would he come? He won't come. My body will remain here. Decomposing. I will be covered in flies. It will be the stink that finally brings him, two or three days later. At first he will only notice the silence. He will knock once. No response. He will push at the door, and it will open easily with a click. On finding my bloody corpse he will panic, aghast at the idea that

136

he might be accused of murdering his tenant. Then he'll see the pistol in my hand and realize that I have committed suicide. He'll run to tell Razmodin.

And then?

Nothing. They'll understand that my suicide was my last sigh at a world that no longer responds to or surprises me.

But, Rassoul, who will say that you've committed such an act? Nobody. Not Yarmohamad, or Razmodin. You know perfectly well that suicide isn't part of your culture. And you know why.

First, in order to commit suicide you have to believe in life, in the value of life. Death has to be worthy of life. Here, in this country, these days, life has no value at all, and therefore neither does suicide.

Next, suicide is considered an ungrateful rebellion against the wishes of Allah. As if you were saying to him: "Here, I'm giving it back before you ask for it, this filthy soul that you introduced into my innocent body!" It's showing that you are more powerful than him, that you won't be his slave, his *banda*. Suicide is giving up your soul, without gratitude.

Before being buried, your body would be whipped. That's why no one admits to suicide. All suicides are disguised as murders. You will merely be a victim, a *shahid*, one martyr among many. You who wanted to be an *Übermensch*.

A *shahid*? No thanks! That's what everyone wants, these days. There'd be no point in that. The whole world would have to know that I had committed suicide.

So, go to a busy crossroads, make a speech and then shoot yourself in the head in front of witnesses. That way everyone will know. But even then, no one will understand the theoretical importance of your act. Each person will create their own explanation. One will say: "He was sick"; another: "He smoked a lot of hashish"; someone else: "It was remorse. He behaved badly toward his family"; or "He regretted being a collaborator, a communist, a traitor!"; and, if they eventually find out that it was you who murdered Nana Alia, they will say that it was your bad conscience that led to your suicide. Yes, no one will say that you committed suicide just because you'd come to the end, that your questions lacked a question mark, that all your questioning had come to nothing more than this stupor faced with the sudden absurdity of life. No one will say that you killed a louse, a loathsome, harmful creature, to attain the status of a "great man" and thus take your place in history. What's more, don't forget that today, here, in this country, everyone wants to attain that status. Everyone is fighting to become either a *ghazi*, if he kills, or a *shahid*, if he is killed. Your nearest and dearest will make you out to be a *ghazi*, because you killed a madam, and a *shahid*, because her family killed you in vengeance. On your tombstone they will write: "*Shahid* Rassoul, son of Ibrahim," whether you want it or not.

No. I don't want that.

Well, then, put down the gun.

So I don't even have the freedom to commit suicide?

No.

Does God really exist, as Dostoevsky said, to prevent man from committing suicide?

That's it, you're off again! No, Rassoul, he was thinking of something else. Your Allah, on the other hand, allows suicide only as a way of bearing witness to his existence and his glory. Any suicide beyond that robs him of his name *Al-Mumit*, he who deals death.

The pistol slips from his hands.

And so it ends. He will not commit suicide, he cannot. Suicide requires just one thing: the action, and nothing more. No thoughts, no words, no remorse, no regret, no hope, no despair . . .

Dawn, bolder than Rassoul, ravages the sky, picking off the stars one by one.

And sleep, more rapacious even than dawn, takes over Rassoul's exhausted body.

A SOFT, gentle murmur ripples through the room, close to him. Through half-open eyes he can only make out a shape: the ethereal face of a wide-eyed young woman. She is whispering: "Rassoul?" It's a lovely dream. "Rassoul!" the voice becomes anxious, loud, forcing him to open his eyes. "Are you OK?"

Sophia? How long has she been here? What time is it? Rassoul stares dully at his Russian alarm clock, which still isn't working—it hasn't worked for ages, he just looks at it out of habit, or "chronic absurdity" as he says.

He sits up and turns toward the window. The sky is still smoky and full of ashes. The sun doesn't know where to appear. It will not appear. It is waiting for the earth to turn.

"What's going on?" asks Sophia, still staring at him anxiously. Rassoul feels for the pistol, and picks it up. "Since when have you been carrying a gun?" she asks suspiciously. He puts it back down so he can pick up a cigarette, making out that he doesn't feel like replying so she doesn't realize that he can't speak, even though he knows how stupid that is. "My mother told me about your father, may God bless his soul. But why didn't you say? Why didn't you go to the burial?" She takes Rassoul's hands in her own. "Now I understand your silence, your sadness . . ." No, Sophia, you don't understand a thing. You ask these questions, when you know that the death of Rassoul's father means nothing to him. It's been a long time that they've been estranged, on both sides. He told you that. He is simply worried for his mother and his sister. He must rescue them. But that too is another story. Rassoul is thinking about one thing and one thing only: Where were you that night? Look at him carefully. Listen to his silence.

"Rassoul, I've gone back to work for Nana Alia." He knows that. "I do love you, I promise, but I have to work. If I don't work, who will? My mother? My brother? You know what our lives are like. I swear to you, when Nazigol came over last night my mother threw herself at her feet, begging to go in my place. But Nazigol wouldn't take her. They don't want her."

They don't want her?

Who is this *they?*

Sophia stifles a sob and continues: "Last time you told me that I shouldn't work there because people would talk, I didn't go. And what happened? A week of starvation, a week of poverty. And who took care of us, that week?" She bursts into tears. "We can't expect anything from you, either. And now you have your mother and sister to look after as well. And you need help yourself. So listen to me. I know it's hard for you to accept, but tell me, Rassoul, do I have any choice?" No, she has no choice. And as she said, Rassoul, you no longer have anything to give her. You are empty. You are nothing. Incapable of suicide, incapable of sorting yourself out, or of protecting your sister and mother; you have even less, therefore, to offer Sophia and her family. You are not ashamed of your hopelessness, your apathy, and yet you feel dishonored and humiliated by what Sophia is doing. She, she is more innocent, purer, more worthy than you. Throw yourself at her feet, and cry out: "*I do not bow down to you, I bow down to all the suffering of humanity.*" Go on!

He trembles.

See, you can't even utter your hero Raskolnikov's most magnificent sentence, but you keep on feigning his nerve. What a wretch!

His hands come together, clasp each other, as if in prayer. His head sinks into his shoulders. He writhes, and is broken. He understands that dignity is neither a stupid manly code of honor nor an absurd tribal morality, but simply the will of a being who admits his own weakness, and demands it be respected.

"Where did this money come from?" asks Sophia, holding out the bundle of notes he gave to Dawoud.

Now you're going to have to write, Rassoul. You can't just stay silent, leaving Sophia in the dark. She'll probably end up thinking that you stole the money from Nana Alia. She and Nazigol must have noticed how strangely you were behaving the other day.

Yes, I'll write it all down for her. This money comes from my mother's sale of my sister Donia to a commandant. It's the price of my cowardice!

More and more agitated, he stands up to look for some paper and a pencil. Sophia stares at him curiously: "You need this money for your mother and your sister . . ." Rassoul finds Sophia's notebook. "I love you, Rassoul. But I can't live with you. Or, rather, you cannot live with me," she says, standing up to put on her chador and leave. But before she walks out of the door Rassoul stops her and hands over the notebook. "What is it? It's . . ." she hesitates, "Is it my notebook?" Yes. "My notebook!" she exclaims vaguely, flooded with memories, smiling shyly. Rassoul gestures that she should open it. She does. He rushes over and turns to the final page, which she reads, rereads quietly to herself, and finally repeats out loud: "*Today, I killed Nana Alia.*" She looks up, not sure she has understood. She walks over to Rassoul. "What does this mean?" He points to the next sentence, and she reads it: "*I killed her for you, Sophia,*" then the next: "*Sophia, I have never kissed you. Do you know why? . . .*" She shuts the notebook, looks down as if searching anywhere but Rassoul's lips for the meaning of the words. "Is it a poem?" she asks candidly. No, I killed. He tries to act it out, in vain. He looks right into her eyes in a fury, a dull fury at his inability to tell her everything. "Stop looking at me like that! You're scaring me. Tell me what it is?" Go on, Rassoul, write down that you've lost your voice. "Why won't you say anything? Have you really decided to stop talking?"

Distraught, he nods "yes," and sits back down on the bed. He almost picks up the pencil and writes, but something stops him. Something cynical. He still doesn't know the cause of this resentment. Probably the fact that his silence annoys everyone, especially those who love him. And yet he does want to tell Sophia, in great detail, exactly how he came up with the idea of killing Nana Alia. It was when they quarreled, a week ago. Afterward he went to the teahouse and heard two militiamen talking about Nana Alia, the filthy whore who wasn't just a moneylender. She had young girls working for her, ostensibly to do the cleaning but in fact for liaisons with her clients. Rassoul suddenly realized why she wanted Sophia to work late into the night. He couldn't bear it. Yes, that was when he had the idea. The next day . . .

"No, you cannot . . . ," she murmurs. "You cannot kill," she repeats, as if she has already heard Rassoul's whole story. She doesn't believe it, will never believe it. Whatever he might say, or rather write, would simply be lying.

Yes, your story is just an absurd pastiche of *Crime and Punishment*, which you've described to her a hundred times, and that's all it is.

Beaten, he looks desperately at Sophia. He would like to ask her why she doesn't believe his story.

But how could she?

There is no proof. No one is talking about it. No one has seen Nana Alia's body, or she would have heard.

That's the thing, I need Sophia's help to unravel the mystery.

It's a mystery to you, but not to her. For her the murder is irrelevant.

She comes up to him, thoughtful and anxious. "Say something to me, Rassoul! Just a word, I'm begging you." What does she want to hear? There is nothing more to say. "Did you really kill her?" Yes. "And you really killed her for me?"

He kneels on his mattress and buries his face in his knees. Sophia bends over and strokes his hair. "Oh Rassoul, you love me that much?"

Yes, he loves you.

She hugs his head. She feels like crying.

Can she live with a murderer?

How to know? She doesn't say anything, either.

But by remaining silent she says a great deal. She says that recently, at Nana Alia's house, she has met only thieves, criminals, and murderers, next to whom Rassoul is merely an innocent little ant. A nothing.

A nothing! He repeats to himself, snuggling deeper into Sophia's arms. And he waits.

He waits for Sophia to instruct him: *Go at once, this very minute, stand at the crossroads, bow down, first kiss the earth which you have defiled and then bow down to all the world and say to all men aloud, "I am a murderer!"*

It would do him good to hear that. But don't forget, Rassoul, that Sophia is not Sonia, Rasknolnikov's sweetheart. Sophia is from another world. She knows that if you do that, in this city, you will be taken for a madman.

"Right, come with me!" she says, disentangling herself from Rassoul and rushing to her chador, which she pulls over her head. "We're going to Shah-e do Shamshira Wali's tomb." But . . . why? "Let's go there, together, to pray. Revive your faith in Allah! Do *tobah*! Tell him that you have killed in his name, and he will forgive you. There are plenty who have killed in his name; you are just one of many."

But I didn't kill in the name of Allah. And I don't need His forgiveness.

So what do you want?

Her to come back to me!

So go with her, follow her!

H E FOLLOWS her.
Wrapped in her sky-blue chador, she walks two steps in front of him. They stride down the big road that leads to the Shah-e do Shamshira Wali mosque and mausoleum, on the banks of the Kabul River. The city is still breathing the sulphurous air of war. Gasping.

They enter the mausoleum courtyard, among the many pilgrims. At the entrance to the tomb Sophia removes her shoes and puts them next to the others, watched by a swarthy caretaker. Rassoul remains outside. He looks for shade beneath the "Wish Tree," whose branches are festooned with countless shreds of colored fabric. An old woman stands up painfully to knot a green ribbon onto the tree. At her feet, an old man sits watching the pigeons ambling around in a pile of grain, making no effort to eat it.

Having managed to tie her ribbon, the old woman sits down triumphantly next to the old man. "My son will come to me, for sure!" The old man isn't listening, he is preoccupied with the pigeons. "Don't give them wheat!" says the old woman crossly. The old man exclaims, "They only eat wheat. People don't understand and bring them millet. Look!" as he throws a handful of wheat to the pigeons, who rush for it. "See?"

"It's a sin!"

"Why is it a sin?"

"Giving wheat is a sin."

"Where did you get that idea?"

"From the Koran."

"Oh?"

"Yes, it was because of wheat that Hazrat Adam and Bibi Hawa were exiled from paradise."

"Show me the verses."

"I told you, it's a sin."

"My sin or their sin?"

"Your sin, it's you who is giving the wheat."

"I don't give a damn. They don't have to eat it, then. They too have their own free will." He is having a good time, and turns toward Rassoul: "Who gives a damn about sin, when you're hungry! Isn't that right?" He leans toward him: "Between you and me, would Hazrat Adam and Bibi Hawa have eaten the forbidden fruit if they weren't hungry? No."

"Don't say that! Don't sin, do not sin . . ." insists the old lady.

"Well, why do you sit here, sharing my sin?" he says. "You wanted to make your wish, you've done it. Your son will come to you. So why are you still here? Go home."

The woman doesn't move.

"Wheat fattens them up. And after all, a fat pigeon is better than a thin one. Do you know why?" the old man asks Rassoul; then, after a moment's pause, to emphasize what he is about to say rather than to wait for a response: "No, you don't know . . ." He looks at Rassoul. "Are you from Kabul?" Yes. "You can't be from here, or you would know why." He takes another handful of wheat from his pocket and holds out his hand so the pigeons will eat from it. "Come on, come here; come and get fat." He asks Rassoul: "Do you make this *ziarat* often?" No. "Good on you. I come here every day. But not to pray, or make a wish. Far from it. I don't look for Allah in tombs. He is here"—he taps his chest—"in my heart!" He moves closer to Rassoul so he can whisper: "You know, the communists spent ten years doing everything they could to turn this nation against Allah, without success. The Muslims, on the other hand, have achieved it in a single year!" and laughs. A silent, mischievous laugh. "You see, all these bearded guys who spend their days praying and moaning over Shah-e do Shamshira Wali's tomb spend their nights doing what the heathens did to that holy man. Do you know his story?" Another pause, once again to emphasize what he's about to say: "No, you don't know it. I'll tell you: he was related to an uncle of the Prophet. This is his sacred tomb. Leys Ben Gheys, the King with two swords! He died a martyr here in Kabul. He had come to convert our country to Islam, and he was killed. He was fighting the unbelievers and they cut off his head; but this holy man continued to fight, with a sword in each hand." The man pauses to observe the effect of his great tale. Shocked by Rassoul's impassivity, he moves closer, lowering his voice as if to share an impressive secret: "Today, the same men who pray here during the day, by night organize ceremonies they call the 'dance of the dead.' Do you know about the 'dance of the dead'?" He stops, glances at Rassoul, and emphasizes: "No, you don't know. I will tell you: they cut off someone's head and splash the wound with boiling oil, making the poor headless body wriggle and hop. They call it the 'dance of the dead.' Had you heard of that? No, you hadn't!" But in fact, old man, Rassoul has heard this story, and others too, worse than that.

The man looks despairingly at the grains of wheat in his trembling hand. From his bloodless lips burst the words: "Do you know . . . why they do it?" No, Rassoul mimes, looking at the man ironically as if to preempt him: "But you're going to tell me." The man searches for the right words, then continues: "Have they no fear of Allah?" They have. And that is why they do it. "Would you be capable of committing an atrocity like that?" Yes. The man is surprised by Rassoul's nod. "You would? Have you no fear of Allah?" No.

The old man's hand is waving about. The grains of wheat fall to the ground. "*Lahawolla belahall* . . . You have no fear of Allah!" and he recites once more his profession of faith. "Are you a Muslim?" Yes.

The man plunges back into his thoughts, re-emerging a few seconds later in still greater despair: "In fact, given everything I've told you, whom should one fear most? Man, or Allah?" And he falls silent.

Surprised by how long Sophia is taking to pray, Rassoul leaves the old man to his doubts and stands up to wander slowly toward the tomb. He stands at the gate and peers inside. A few women are keening as they lean over the rails surrounding the tomb. Others have sat down to pray in silence. Sophia is not among them. He returns to the caretaker and looks for her shoes, but cannot find them.

He glances back inside. No sign of her. Nor outside, either.

What has happened? Why did this heart, which had once again opened, shut back down so quickly? Did she bring him here to distance herself from him, to bid him goodbye, without a word?

G OODBYE, SOPHIA!
And he takes a great drag of hash, which he holds in his lungs for as long as possible.

Goodbye, Sophia! You left with the only secret I had. Goodbye!

Another two or three drags, and he leaves the *saqi-khana*.

I am never coming back. I'm going to shut myself in my room, as gloomy as a grave, with no future and no way out. I will not eat. I will not drink. I will not leave my bed. I will let myself be taken by an endless sleep, free of dreams and of thought. Until I am nothing. A nothingness in the emptiness, a shadow in the abyss, an immortal corpse.

When he reaches the courtyard he finds Dawoud sitting on the steps. "Hello, Rassoul. My mother sent me to fetch you. Sophia is not well. She has shut herself in her bedroom and won't see anyone."

It was she who fell into my abyss.

He leaps down the stairs, dashes across the courtyard and runs through the streets. Arriving at Sophia's house out of breath, he rushes straight to her bedroom door.

"She's crying. She won't speak. She's locked herself in . . ." says the mother. She bangs on the door. "Sophia! Rassoul-*djan* has come." A long silence, then the sound of a key turning in the lock. The mother opens the door and lets Rassoul in first.

Sophia returns to her bed and huddles up, her head on her knees. The silence is oppressive; the mother can sense that the couple need to be alone. She leaves, with a final, damning glance at Rassoul. Has Sophia told her everything?

No, she can't have. She will have kept my secret. Not only to protect me, but to prevent her mother's suffering. She doesn't want to share my abyss with anyone else. But she must not sink; she must not suffer in there. I will get her out.

He kneels next to Sophia and, after a brief hesitation, shyly strokes her hand.

Don't be afraid, Sophia. I'm not your typical murderer. I am . . .

"They ran me out of the mausoleum!" she says in a hopeless voice. He lets go of her hand, annoyed. "One of Nana Alia's neighbors was there. When she saw me, she went and spoke to the caretaker, and he threw me out . . ." Why . . . The word trembles on Rassoul's lips; it emerges as a breath, a silent breath, lacking a question mark; a mute cry of despair. From now on, he

153

mustn't be surprised when people treat Sophia with contempt, as a prostitute.

She is crying.

Rassoul feels himself falter.

"I left quietly. Without telling you. I didn't want you to make a scene," she says, as if Rassoul would have been capable.

No, Sophia, Rassoul has changed. Look at him. He is lost, trapped inside his pitiful rage.

No, he may have sunk to a terrible low, but he still has his dignity.

So move, Rassoul, move!

He stands up suddenly and leaves the room. Sophia's mother is standing on the patio, by the window. As soon as she sees him she turns her head away to hide her tears.

In the street, there is no shade. The sun streaks through the smoke to beat down on peoples' heads with its massive midday power.

Rassoul walks with his head hung low. He makes it home without knowing how. The room smells awful; it's the cheese.

He has no desire to get rid of it. He grabs the pistol that is still lying on the floor, and checks the cartridge. It is still loaded. He puts the pistol in his pocket and leaves the room.

Where is he going?

Nowhere. He's walking. Going wherever the pistol takes him.

May he no longer think about anything!

He is no longer thinking. He thinks nothing about anything.

He sees only the road,

follows only the shadow crushed under his feet,

sees no face,

hears no sound,

heeds no cry,

receives no laugh.

He walks.

He counts his steps.

Stop right here, in front of the Shah-e do Shamshira Wali mausoleum.

Everything is quiet. The pilgrims and beggars have all left. Rassoul enters the courtyard and approaches the tomb. Rosewater masks the smell of pigeons and the sulphur of war. The caretaker has fallen asleep on a bench in the shade of the Wish Tree. One hand under his chin, the other on his chest. He looks as innocent as a sleeping child. His salt and pepper beard quivers from time to time, like that of a goat before the sacrifice. Rassoul walks toward him, pulls out his pistol, moves even closer and takes aim. His finger tightens on the trigger. His hand shakes. He hesitates.

Killing someone as they sleep; now that is cowardice. What's more, his death would be very quick. He would not suffer at all. He must not die without knowing what he has done, in the innocence of sleep.

Let him wake, so he can know why I am killing him. So he can suffer!

He will suffer, yes, for a few seconds; but the reason for his death will die with him. No one will say that this caretaker was killed because he chased Sophia from the mausoleum, because he closed the house of Allah to a "public girl" who'd come here to pray, to beg forgiveness for her fiancé . . . So, Rassoul, you would be committing another pointless murder. Failing, again.

The sun works its way through the branches and leaves of the Wish Tree, dappling the body of the caretaker, as well as Rassoul's feet, legs and hair, and the Colt that trembles in his hands. Drenched in sweat and crushed by doubt, he crouches in front of the caretaker and, after a few moments of complete inertia, takes out a cigarette. None of the sounds that he makes disturb the old man's sleep. Is he hard of hearing? Or does Rassoul not exist?

He backs away, but a sudden muffled noise from behind roots him to the spot. He spins around. It's a cat.

A cat, at the mausoleum? Its presence here is strange, and Rassoul watches it approach, brush his foot with its raised tail, and slip silently into the shadow of the caretaker who slowly awakes. Rassoul starts. He tosses away his cigarette and resumes his aim, blinking. The man's sleepy gaze shows no fear. He doesn't even move. Perhaps he thinks he is dreaming. Rassoul moves closer, gesturing for him to sit up. But the man just reaches calmly under the rug covering the bench to pick up a bowl of money, which he holds out to Rassoul.

This man hasn't understood anything. I am not a thief. I am here to kill him.

He walks closer, moving his lips to form silent words: "And do you know why I am killing you?"

No, Rassoul, he doesn't know, and he will never know.

Rassoul's hand is trembling with rage.

Even now the caretaker doesn't react. He remains unruffled. He puts the bowl back in its place, smiles and closes his eyes in anticipation of the shot. Rassoul pokes him with the barrel of the gun. The man opens his eyes again, slowly. He is still impassive, even though the pistol is now held at his temple. His gaze, just like that of the donkey in Nayestan, says to Rassoul: What are you waiting for? Shoot! If you don't kill me, a rocket will. I would prefer to die at your hands, protecting the purity and glory of this sacred place. I will die a *shahid*.

A woman concealed by a sky-blue chador enters the courtyard. She sees Rassoul with his gun held to the caretaker's head, turns, and flees.

He still doesn't dare shoot.

No, I don't want this man to die a martyr.

He throws down the pistol.

And leaves.

ET LOST! There's nothing here anymore," grumbles a cavernous voice. But Rassoul keeps banging on the door of the *saqi-khana,* and in the end it fearfully cracks open. "Is that you, Rassoul? You should have said!" exclaims Hakim. "Which Rassoul is it, the holy man or the pothead?" asks Kaka Sarwar as usual, his voice seeping out along with the smell and the smoke.

Rassoul enters and finds a place among the circle of men; the same men, all keeping a solemn silence as they stare at Kaka Sarwar, who is smoking greedily. Rassoul looks around for Jalal. He is no longer there to ask if the war has started yet. It's Mustapha who asks, breaking the languor of the circle. Others shush him. Silence again, still solemn, still focused on Kaka Sarwar. Everyone is waiting for him to pass on the pipe and continue the tale that Rassoul's arrival has interrupted. "Should I start again at the beginning?"

"No, just keep going!" cries everyone at once.

"But this young man wasn't here!"

"We'll tell him the beginning later."

"OK," he says, and passes the chillum. "Where was I? I've lost my thread . . ."

"You found yourself in a village . . ."

"That's right. And what a village! Houses carved out of wood, with no windowpanes, no doors, and no courtyard walls. I could hear voices, but couldn't see anyone. The houses were empty. Or rather the darkness prevented me from seeing anyone or anything. There were only voices, nothing but voices, orchestral, harmonious, peaceful voices. They were coming from a semi-ruined cave on the edge of the village, at the foot of a rocky, steep, arid hill. All the villagers were there, dancing in a trance. Men and women. Young, old, children. The men wore vine leaves on their heads; the women's *shushuts* were embroidered with cowries and red pearls. They were handing out drinks to everyone."

"Were they unbelievers?"

"I've no idea. They were all drinking and singing. My presence didn't disturb them at all; it was as if I didn't exist. They even served me drinks, without a single question; first a vibrant yellow liquid called 'stone saw'; then a bright red one called 'stone file.' The first was sour; the second bitter." Kaka Sarwar pauses again to smoke. "I drank a lot that night! And nobody seemed to want to know why I was there. Once I had identified their leader, who was a woman, I went to see her. I had barely said hello when she greeted me and asked: 'Are you lost, young man?' I shyly admitted that I was. With a friendly smile, she welcomed me to the 'Valley of Lost Words.' She asked me where I was going, and where I had come from. Once I had told her everything she nodded, offered me a final glass of 'stone file' and called over an old man to take me to the neighboring village. He gave me a storm lamp, and off we went. He walked confidently and fast. I rushed to light the path in front of him, but he told me to keep the lamp for myself as he didn't need it. Panting, I asked him how it was that they had a woman as leader. As we walked, he told me an incredible story that I will tell you all tomorrow."

"No, now! Come on!" they all protested. Kaka Sarwar turned toward Hakim: "But I'm hungry."

"We'll buy you a kebab and some tea. Who has money?"

Nobody moved except Rassoul, who took a high-value note out of his pocket and gave it to Hakim.

"You will never be bankrupt!" Kaka Sarwar blessed him. "So I will tell the rest of the story to you. But first, the chillum!" They gave it to him; he smoked and passed it to Rassoul. "This woman, the head of the village, was the descendant of a great sage among sages, who lived a long time ago in a faraway kingdom. He was blind, but able to read manuscripts simply by caressing the letters with the tip of his finger. Misfortune hit him one day when people noticed that, as he read, the words were slowly being erased from the book." He stops and stares at the enthralled faces around him. After a deep breath, he takes the chillum once more. The smoke muffles his voice: "Poets, holy men, judges . . . all were panicking. They hid their manuscripts for fear that they would be read by this blind sage. And they forced the king to banish him from the kingdom. The sage and his whole family went into exile against their will. He settled in the valley I was telling you about. He built a city where everyone learned everything by heart. They didn't have a single book, nothing was written down. Because they knew it all. Books are made for idiots!" He bursts out laughing, then smokes, coughs, and continues: "They invented a new language, one impossible to forget. From then on storytellers, poets, and holy men flocked to this valley from all over the world so that the people would translate their work, bring it to life in their voices, and immortalize it in their memories. It is said that in this place even stories that had been forgotten—true and false, known and unknown—came back to people's minds, took shape once more, reconnected to the voices of the storytellers . . . And this was, of course, threatening to the history distorters, the tale forgers, the falsifiers of secrets, the science imposters, the shady politicians . . . One day, they all descended upon the village. Invaded and destroyed it. They destroyed everything! They deafened the children and cut out the adults' tongues. But . . ." a pause, a long drag on the chillum, "but what they didn't realize was that in this valley there were not only human beings. The houses, the trees, the rocks, the water, the wind, the air, the birds, the snakes . . . everything in this valley could remember the people, its history, its wisdom, and also the barbarism of the tyrants!" His voice gathers pace, trembles. "Yes, everything can be destroyed, but never memory, or memories. Never!" He falls silent and withdraws from the circle to lean against the wall.

"What happened then?" asks Mustapha, seemingly bewitched.

"What do you mean, then?"

"To you?"

"To me? Oh, yes!" exclaims Kaka Sarwar, moving away from the wall. Serene once more, he continues: "My guide finished the story about his leader just as we entered the neighboring village. He left me at a hidden shrine where I could spend the night. As I gave him back his storm lamp, as I shook his hand and thanked him, I noticed that he was blind!"

"You're kidding!" cries Mustapha, astounded. Another young man objects: "Kaka Sarwar, you invented this story. It never happened. It isn't true!"

"But now it is—as a holy man among holy men from the land of the setting sun used to say—*because I have told it to you*," retorts Kaka Sarwar with a mischievous smile.

"Where do you get all these stories, Kaka Sarwar?"

"From the Valley of Lost Words, my son."

"So it really does exist, then!" exclaims Mustapha.

Another few drags: the dry tongue, the hacking cough setting fire to the chest, the blood freezing in the veins, the heart beating slowly, and the whole body flying.

*　　*　　*

At that point Rassoul stands up, steadies himself against the wall and leaves the smoking den.

Outside, the city is a furnace. Everything is rippling in the heat: the mountain, the houses, the stones, the trees, the sun . . . Everything is quaking with fear. Except Rassoul. He is light, soothed. He walks the streets like the last man on earth, unable to catch a single eye, caress a single soul, or hear a single word. He feels like crying out that he is the last man, that the others are all dead, dead to him; and then to start running, and laughing . . . all the way to the Larzanak bridge.

The bridge shakes with the explosion of a rocket not far away. But Rassoul doesn't move. He does not drop to the floor. He just stands there, as if daring the gunmen to launch their rockets at him. Go on, fire! I am here. And I'll remain here, in front of you. You—so deaf, so blind, so mute!

Dust envelops the river, the bridge, the body, the gaze, the voice . . .

He continues on his way, passing in front of the Hotel Metropole. It is chaos in there, too. Foreign journalists, hotel employees, and armed bearded men are all running around in a frenzy. Perhaps Razmodin is back. Rassoul enters the lobby.

A young employee—the one who came to find Rassoul in the *saqi-khana*—is busy transporting a wounded foreign journalist. When he sees Rassoul he stops and removes the couple of dollars clenched between his teeth: "Razmodin is not here. He has disappeared. He left yesterday, we haven't seen him since. Everyone is getting out. There's going to be . . ." A violent explosion just opposite rocks the building. The wounded journalist is crying. He gives another dollar to the young man, who quickly carries him down to the basement.

Outside, everyone is shooting, without knowing at whom or what for.

Shooting.
  Shooting . . .
  The bullet will find its target.

R ASSOUL DRAGS himself outside, with no particular destination in mind and indifferent to the chaos of the city. He has no desire to return to Sophia's house, or to visit his aunt in search of Razmodin—who must be in Mazar anyway, with Donia. He walks toward the Ministry of Information and Culture. From behind a barricade someone shouts: "Watch out, *khar-koss*!"

Rassoul heads for the voice. A man grabs him and pulls him to safety, scolding: "You fucking idiot! If you've had enough of this life, go and die somewhere else; we don't have time to dispose of your body. Where the hell are you going?" It is Jano's friend, the one who beat him up in his room. "If you're looking for Commandant Parwaiz, he's not here. He's gone to look for Jano, who's disappeared."

Jano disappeared? He must have fled. He must have had enough of the war.

Rassoul stands up and moves away from the barricade. He wanders through the shouting, the shooting, the tanks . . . and nothing hits him. He makes it to Zarnegar Park. Smoke hangs amid the trees. He stretches out on the grass in a corner of the park. He smokes, nonchalantly adding his cigarette smoke to that of the gunfire. He closes his eyes and lies there for a good long while. Gradually the noise fades into a prolonged and profound silence.

Suddenly, there is the sound of footsteps approaching, skimming his head, gently penetrating his lifeless state. He opens his eyes. A woman draped in a sky-blue chador is passing right by him. At the sight of her he sits up.

Sophia.

He gets to his feet and begins hesitantly to follow her.

When the woman notices she is being shadowed she slows down, stops, and turns fearfully toward Rassoul. She moves aside to let him pass. But he stops walking too. Disconcerted, she sets off again.

Leave her alone, Rassoul. It isn't Sophia.

But who is it, then?

Just a woman, one of so many.

But what is she doing here? Why has she come to the park, especially now, when everyone is running to safety?

Like you, she is taking refuge in the park, protecting herself among the trees.

No, she has come to see me. I'm sure of it.

The woman reaches the edge of the park and takes the main road toward Malekazghar junction.

Rassoul speeds up, overtakes her and bars her way.

She stops, afraid. She looks around wildly but there's

no one in sight. Increasingly terrified, she edges past Rassoul to continue silently on her way. Rassoul follows her. Now that she is close, he tries to see if she's the same size as Sophia. No. What about Nana Alia's daughter? Hard to tell. So why are you following her?

I don't know. It's strange that she came here. She must be looking for someone.

But not you!

Who knows?

They reach the junction. She crosses it quickly.

Look at her. Is she behaving like someone who has come to find you? It seems more as if she's running away.

Disappointed, he gives up the chase and lights a cigarette.

But once she reaches the other side of the junction, the woman stops and turns to look at Rassoul.

She's playing with me. She is expecting me to follow her.

And he sets off to catch her up. She rushes away again.

"Stop!"

Rassoul stops.

Where did that voice come from?

From you!

"Stop!"—yes, it came out of my mouth!

He cries: "Stop!" It is definitely his voice, fragile, damaged, muffled, but audible. "Stop!" He breaks into a run. The woman runs too. "Stop!" He catches her up, breathless. "Stop! I . . . I've got my voice back!" He tries to make out the woman's face through the grille of her chador. "I can speak!" He moves a step closer. "I want to speak to you." She is listening. He searches for the right words.

"Who are you?" She says nothing. "Who sent you?"

His hand, more shaky even than his voice, reaches out to lift her veil. The woman steps back, frightened. "Whoever you are, you must know me. You came to find me. You came to make me speak. Didn't you?" The woman looks away. "In my dream, it was you who brought me my Adam's apple." He touches her. She shivers, and backs away.

"I know you. I was looking for you. You're the woman in the sky-blue chador. I recognized your walk. It was you who saw Nana Alia's body, and made it disappear. You left with her jewelry box and her money. You did a good job. You are shrewd, and clever. Well done!" She starts to cross the street, on to the other pavement. "You need to know something: I could have killed you, as well, but I chose not to. You owe me your life, did you know that?" She totters—from fear, or exhaustion—steadies herself, and rushes off. "Listen to me! Wait a minute. I've so much to say to you." She steps off the pavement and stands in the middle of the road, hoping to see something arrive—a car, a tank—but there is nothing. Nobody. Rassoul is chasing after her.

"Don't run away. I won't hurt you. I couldn't." He grabs at her chador, which slips between his fingers. "You can't run away from me anymore. It's over. We have found each other. We share a life, a destiny.

We are the same. The two of us have dirtied our hands with the same crime. I killed; you stole. I'm a murderer; you're a traitor . . ." The woman stops, turns around to stare at him, and rushes off again. Surprised by this unexpected pause, Rassoul continues more calmly: "And yet this crime that we share weighs on my conscience only. It's not fair that I'm the only one to suffer. I who committed the murder in order to free my fiancée from that whore, and use her money to save both our families. If only I had the money and the jewels; instead, I'm haunted by remorse. Help me! Only you can help me. We could join forces, keep this secret until the end of our days, and be happy." The woman slows down once more—thinking, deliberating, or just resting—and then continues on her way toward Kabul Wellayat, the governor's office. "Tell me what you've done with the jewels and the money. They belong to me. I must have them. They would ensure the happiness of two families—or even three, if we include yours. Who cares if they arrest me, who cares if they hang me; at least I will be relieved of my crime. I will be finished with all this suffering." The woman, still silent, walks along the outside of the Kabul Wellayat. Rassoul dares go no further. He stares at the woman. "Take me with you, or I will tell the police at the governor's office. Do you hear me, you deaf, dumb creature?" Still silence. "At least tell me who you are. Tell me if my crime has made you happy." The woman reaches the gate of the Wellayat, stops, and turns toward Rassoul as if to invite him inside. He sidles hesitantly along the wall. "No, you can't be happy without me. You need me, like I need you. We are like Adam and Eve. Two sides of the same coin. Both of us driven out to live on this cursed earth. We can't live without each other. We are condemned to share our crime, and our punishment. We will create a family. Travel far, far away, to the remotest of valleys. We will build a city that we will call . . . the 'Valley of Lost Sins.' We will invent our own laws, our own morality. And we will have children—not like Cain and Abel, or else I will kill Cain. Yes, I will kill him because I know his potential. I will kill him the moment he is born!" The woman opens the gate and, after a final glance at Rassoul, enters the courtyard. He stands there astounded. He looks around; the street is still deserted; the silence is deeper than ever; the sky, low and heavy. He walks right up to the gate of the Wellayat. Through the grill, he can see only the ruins, and no trace of the woman.

Who was she?

W HO'S THERE?" A high-pitched voice stops Rassoul in his tracks. Where did it come from? He calls out, in his fragile, feeble voice: "Is anyone there?"

"Yes, djinns!" resounds another voice, prompting sarcastic laughter from a stone sentry box by the Kabul Wellayat gate. Peering inside, Rassoul can just discern two bodies stretched out on the ground. "Did you see a woman go in?"

"A woman? Here? If only!" The two bodies shake with laughter.

"Is there anyone at the Wellayat?"

"Who do you want?"

"The public prosecutor."

"Which djinn is that?' And then, to his mate, "Do you know it?"

"No. Ask him for a cigarette."

Rassoul takes two cigarettes and holds them out. "Throw them in!" He obeys, insisting: "There must be someone there, though? A governor, a judge, or . . ."

"Go and see for yourself! Why ask us?"

*   *   *

171

Rassoul didn't see the soldiers' faces. He makes his way into the ransacked courtroom, its floor strewn with charred papers and notebooks. The walls are riddled with bullets. The governor's chair is empty, engulfed in a dense, doleful silence. There is still no trace of the woman in the sky-blue chador.

A strange appearance!

A strange disappearance.

An ethereal woman, appearing out of nowhere as if to give him back his voice, show him the way, deliver him to the law, and bring him here, to the Kabul Wellayat, where everything is in ruins: not only the law courts but also the "surveillance" building and prison.

He stops in front of the only building in decent condition. He walks up the stairs and through the door, into a long passage with filthy walls. His steps ring out, making the silence even more intense and foreboding. Suddenly he stops in his tracks, gripped by a strange sensation. He hesitates, then continues against his better judgment. The doors off the passage are open, allowing some light into the dark and squalid little box-rooms on either side. Despite a few tables, chairs and other office furniture, these rooms are all completely soulless— except one, where a few items of women's and children's clothing are hanging from a washing line in the sunlight. They are still wet; so there is life here. The woman in the sky-blue chador must live in this room.

I'm going to meet her at last!

Halfway down the passage Rassoul hears footsteps,

and then a small boy appears from the basement stairs. As soon as he sees Rassoul he runs down again. Rassoul follows him into the basement, where a sign says: "Law Archives." A dim light at the end of a long corridor beckons him to a room from which muffled, senile whispers can be heard: "You . . . Younness . . . Youss . . . Youssef . . ." Rassoul enters the room. It is large, and lined with cupboards and shelves stuffed full of old, yellowing files. The voice still emanates from somewhere out of sight. "Is anyone there?" he calls shyly. No response, just the senile voice rambling on: "Youssef . . ."

"Is anyone there?" he asks again, almost shouting this time. After a pause, the same voice replies: "Not one, but two of us!" then continues: "Youssef, Youssef, Youssef K . . ." as if chanting an incantation. Rassoul searches for a way to get to the man. He finds him standing at the far end of the room, in front of a small basement window and behind a large desk. He is rummaging through files as a boy holds up a lamp for him to see.

They both look up at the sound of Rassoul's footsteps. The old man nods as if in greeting, then mechanically returns to his work. Rassoul walks up to the desk and says: "I'm looking for the public prosecutor."

The old man, leafing through a large notebook he has extracted from one of the files, doesn't seem to have heard him. He turns a few pages, and then starts moving his finger down a list of names. "Youssef . . . Ka, Youssef

173

Kab . . . Youssef Kabuli! Isn't that him, son?" The boy holding the lamp is distracted by Rassoul's presence. The old man grumbles: "I'm talking to you, boy; look and see if this is your father's name. What's the matter with you?" The boy, unsettled, bends to look at the notebook. Rassoul takes a step forward and asks again, impatiently: "Where can I find the prosecutor?"

"I heard you, *mohtaram*. I understood what you were asking. You didn't pose a riddle, as far as I can tell!" A pause, to obtain Rassoul's agreement, and then he asks: "Is it urgent?" in an intimidating voice that makes Rassoul hesitate before muttering that it is.

"Let me finish this case, and then I'll get to yours," says the old man before turning grumpily to the boy: "So, do you know how to read or not?"

"Yes, I can read, but your finger . . ."

"What about my finger?"

"It's covering it."

"I'm telling you to read the name above my finger, you cretin!" The boy looks down and drones: "You, Yous . . . Youssef . . . Ka, Kabuli, yes, that's it, I think."

"You think? You've been hassling me about this name for a week, and now you're not sure! This is serious, son, most serious."

"I'm not saying I'm not sure. I'm saying I think so."

"What are you rambling on about? Oh well. What's the file number, anyway?"

"The file number?"

"Yes, the numbers!"

174

"The numbers? . . . There aren't any numbers. See for yourself!"

"What do you mean there aren't any numbers? Lift up the lamp!" The boy lifts the lamp and the weary old man yells: "So how am I supposed to find this bloody file, then?" and stares at the pile of papers.

"Before going back to your search, do you think you could reply to me about whether the honorable prosecutor . . ." Rassoul asks testily.

"Listen to me, young man: this boy's case is far more important than the presence or absence of the prosecutor! A family's fate hangs in the balance. I've been busting a gut for a week now to get my hands on this file, and you want me to drop it all to look for the honorable prosecutor! First, there no longer is a prosecutor. Second, this is not a reception. This is the office of the Law Archives. And I am merely a humble clerk who is now, for my sins, in charge of this place!" He pauses a moment, then bends back over the list of names and mutters: "What do you want with the bloody prosecutor, anyway?"

"I've come to hand myself over to the law."

"Oh, sorry, there's no one to receive you."

Stunned but also annoyed, Rassoul moves closer and tries to talk calmly, in his broken voice: "I did not come to be received. I came to . . ." He raises his voice as if to spell out every word: "TO HAND MYSELF OVER TO THE LAW!"

"I understand. I too hand myself over to the law every morning. As does this young man."

"But I have come to be arrested. I'm a criminal."

"Well, come back tomorrow. There's no one here today." He returns to his big book. Rassoul is spitting with rage; he puts a hand on top of the pile of papers and howls from his emaciated throat: "Did you hear what I said? Have you understood what I want?"

"Yes, I did! You've come to hand yourself over to the law, because you are a criminal. Is that it?"

Rassoul stares at him, dumbfounded. The man nods his head and asks, "So?"

"So, you must arrest me."

"But I can't do anything for you. As I've said, I'm just the court clerk."

"Give me some money, *baba*, so I can buy some bread." The voice of a child emerges from behind the shelves, attracting the attention of all three men. It's the same boy that Rassoul saw earlier, in the passage.

"I'll go . . ." says the young man, son of Youssef Kabuli.

"No. You stay here, we're looking for your father," instructs the clerk as he gives the child some money. Then he turns back to his big notebook, grumbling. "They say I'm the clerk, but actually I do everything around here. There are no trials these days, so I focus on the archives instead . . ." He is still leafing through the notebook. "I swear the rats would have gnawed through all these files by now if I weren't here. Or else they would have been destroyed by bombs."

"Yes, that's true, it's swarming with rats down here!"

confirms the young man as he puts away the files on the instructions of the clerk.

Troubled by the clerk's flippancy, Rassoul takes out a cigarette and lights it. His desperate voice becomes hoarse: "I've killed someone." Neither of them takes any notice. Perhaps they didn't hear. So he repeats more loudly, to make sure. "I've killed someone." Both of them turn to look at him, but immediately and soundlessly return to their work.

Perhaps they heard, but didn't understand.

He is finding it hard to speak. His voice is still muffled, barely audible.

He raises his voice and shouts: "But have you understood?" The clerk glares at him, but doesn't reply. Again the silence, the heads bent over the files, the names, the numbers, the doubts . . . And Rassoul continuing, as if to himself: "I know it is no great achievement, I know I have not done anything terribly unusual. But that doesn't matter. I have killed, and now I have come to hand myself over to the law." With that, he sits down at the foot of a cupboard.

Rassoul's stubborn presence weighs increasingly on the old clerk, who finally closes the large notebook. "Farzan, we will continue looking for your father tomorrow. Go and make some tea," he says to the young man, who immediately puts the lamp on the table and asks excitedly: "Green or black?"

"Green or black?" repeats the clerk, turning to Rassoul.

"Black," replies Rassoul wearily.

Farzan leaves. The old clerk picks up the lamp and walks over to the shelves. "That poor Farzan. Under the monarchy his father was a highly skilled accountant, and they were a respectable family. But then the communists came for the father, arrested him and sent him to prison without explanation. What was his crime? No one has ever been told and, as with all prisoners in that era, there was never any trial. They lost track of him. People said he was hanged, or exiled to Siberia. No one knows for sure what happened to him. And now his son is obsessed with finding out what became of his father. He wants to know what he was accused of. I know he will never succeed." He returns to the desk. "In my opinion, the day the father was arrested something serious happened in the family, which the son has been trying to uncover and understand ever since. And that is what interests me, too. Not the rest of it—justice, injustice, etc. Those are only preferences, not philosophies." He pauses for a moment to observe how Rassoul responds to his maxim, before continuing: "Since he started coming here, he has become my assistant . . . ," he chuckles. "I still love collecting stories about the law. They help one understand the history of a country, the character of a people. I have thousands of them. I need time to write them out. But nobody gives me that time. Look!" He points to a mound of files in one corner. "The supreme judge asked me for a list of all the mujahideen imprisoned during the communist era, and also a list of all the *shahids*. They say that the Ministry of

Shahids is asking for it. The Ministry of Shahids!" He starts chuckling again, ironically this time, glancing at Rassoul who is staring sadly at a rat trap beneath the desk.

"So, young man, who did you kill?"

"A woman."

"And were you in love with her?" he asks, continuing to tidy his papers.

IN OUR dear legal system, killing a madam is not murder . . . So . . . so something else must be causing you this distress." The clerk settles into his chair and stares intensely at Rassoul, who looks down and arduously swallows a small piece of bread. All three of them are sitting around the desk, transformed into a tea table. "To summarize: you are worrying, feeling completely distraught, because you can't understand why your murder is shrouded in such mystery. Is that right?"

"Yes, but . . ."

"As I was saying, when I first heard your story, I thought you were suffering because you'd made such a mess of it; because you hadn't taken the money and the jewels, which would have allowed you to save your family. Then you realized that if you did have the money and jewels belonging to Nana . . . what's her name? Yes, that's right, Nana Alia . . . you would feel even more haunted by remorse and regret. With hindsight, you see that the money and the jewels were just a pretext. Really, you killed that madam to wipe a cockroach off the face of the earth, and most of all to avenge your fiancée. But now you recognize that it didn't change a thing. The murder didn't ease your thirst for vengeance. It didn't comfort you. On the contrary, it created an abyss into which you are plunging deeper every day . . . So what is tormenting you now is neither the failure of your crime nor the guilt of your conscience; rather, you are suffering from the futility of your act. In short, you are the victim of your own crime. Am I right?"

"Yes, that's it, I am the victim of my own crime. And the worst thing is that not only was my crime banal and futile, it doesn't exist. No one is talking about it. The body has mysteriously disappeared. Everyone thinks Nana Alia has just gone to the countryside, taking her money and her jewels with her. Have you ever, in all your legal archives, come across such an absurd case?"

"Oh, young man, I've seen crimes far more absurd than yours. And I have also seen that killing a madam doesn't eradicate evil from the world. Especially these days. As you have said, in this country killing is the most insignificant act there is."

"That's why I've come to hand myself over to the law. I want to give my crime some meaning."

"And have you given your life meaning, before you try to give some to your crime?"

"That's exactly what I was trying to do with this murder."

"Like all those who kill in the name of Allah so as to forget their sins! That's nonsense, young man, nonsense! Do you understand?"

181

"Yes." Rassoul nods before asking the clerk: "Have you read Dostoevsky?"

"No. Is he Russian?"

"Yes, he's a Russian author, but not a communist. Anyway, that isn't the point. He said that if God didn't exist . . ."

"*Tobah na'ouzobellah!* May Allah protect you from this deviance! Drive out that devilish thought!"

"Yes, may Allah forgive me! This Russian said—*Tobah na'ouzobellah*—that if God didn't exist . . . everything would be permitted." After a thoughtful silence, the clerk says: "He wasn't wrong!" and murmurs into Rassoul's ear: "So, how would your precious Russian explain the fact that here, today, in your dear country, everyone believes in Allah the Merciful yet all atrocities are permitted?"

"You're saying that these people . . ." interrupts Farzan, bewildered by the turn of the conversation.

"You, boy, go and fetch the water!" instructs the clerk expediently, before continuing: "You know, we say that if sin exists, it is because God exists."

"Yes, but these days it seems to me that it's the other way round. May Allah forgive me! If he exists, it is not to prevent sins, but to justify them."

"Well, yes, sadly. We are always using him, and History, and Conscience, and ideologies to justify our crimes and our betrayals. Rare are those who, like you, commit a crime and then feel remorse."

"Oh, no! I don't feel remorse."

"OK then, not remorse. But you are aware of your crime. Take a look around: Who isn't killing? And how many criminals have arrived at your level of awareness? Not one."

"Exactly. It is my awareness that creates my guilt."

"In that case why do you need a trial or a sentence? Legal proceedings—in an ideal world—are for those who don't recognize their crime or guilt. And in any case, who could judge you, now? There is no one here, no judge and no public prosecutor. Everyone is at war. Everyone is chasing after power. They have neither the time nor the inclination to come and administer your trial. They are even afraid of trials. The trial of one person can lead to that of others. Do you understand what I'm saying?" Rassoul is confused. The clerk continues: "What do you want? To be imprisoned? Your soul is imprisoned in your body, and your body in this city."

"So, it makes no difference whether I'm in here or outside."

"It makes no difference."

"In that case, I'm staying here."

The clerk has had enough. He picks up the file and throws it on the floor. "But there's no one here. I can't deal with you," he cries, "there's no more prison, no more 'surveillance' department . . . nothing. There is nothing here anymore! Not even the law. They are busy altering the penal code. It will all be based on *fiqh*, on sharia." He stares furiously at Rassoul for a long time, in oppressive silence. Then, before picking up the file lying at Rassoul's feet, he holds out his hand: "Delighted to have met you, young man. It's time for my prayers. Good day!" He puts the file back on the desk, and withdraws into another room.

Rassoul is staggered—wordless, voiceless, more mute than before.

Where am I?

In *Nakodja abad,* nowhere land!

Farzan returns. "So you're staying? Good decision. It's great, here. It's a safe haven . . . Mr Clerk Sir lives here with his whole family. It's nice and cool. His wife is lovely. She's very pretty, too, and a good cook . . ."

"The woman who came in just before I did? A woman in a sky-blue chador?"

"Oh, no! She never goes out. She's afraid of the bombs. She's afraid of being alone. She's a bit . . ."

So she isn't that wretched woman. In that case, why is the clerk so keen for me to leave?

"Brother!" A deep voice, followed by footsteps finding their way in the dark, interrupts Rassoul's suspicious thoughts. Farzan dashes into the next-door room, signaling for Rassoul to follow, but he doesn't. Four armed men appear.

"Isn't the clerk here?"

"He is praying," replies Rassoul.

"And you, what are you doing here?" asks one.

"My name is Rassoul, and I have come to hand myself over to the law."

"What are you doing?" asks the same man. "Are you working here?" continues another. "No, I have come to hand myself over to the law," repeats Rassoul, dazed by these four men who keep exchanging suspicious glances. One of them says, "We're not hiring, you know!"

"I haven't come to work. I've come to be tried." One of the men strokes his beard and stares at Rassoul. "You want to be tried? For what?"

"I've killed someone."

They look at each other again. Uneasy. They don't know what to say. In the end, one of them walks up to Rassoul and says: "We'll have to check this out with Qhazi sahib. Come with us!"

As they are leaving the building, the clerk comes up with Farzan in tow. "You were looking for me?"

"Yes, Qhazi sahib wants to know if you have his list of *shahids*."

"Not yet!"

"Go back to work, then, and bring it to us as soon as you do!" But the clerk just stands there, aghast at Rassoul's idiocy.

They enter a partially destroyed building, and then an imposing room furnished with a large desk. The judge is sitting behind it, paying them absolutely no mind and eating a large slice of watermelon. A white cap covers his great shaved head; a long beard lengthens his fleshy face. They wait for him to finish. Finally, he puts the

185

rind down on a tray, takes out a large handkerchief, and wipes his mouth, beard, and hands. With a stomach-settling belch, he motions to an old man to take away the tray. Then he picks up his prayer beads, glances at Rassoul, and asks the others: "What's the problem?"

"We have brought you a murderer." The Qhazi's gaze moves from Rassoul to his men with no expression except for a silent "So?"

"Where did you arrest him?"

"We didn't arrest him. He turned himself in." Now the judge is surprised. He looks back at Rassoul. "Who did he kill?" No response. One of the men murmurs in Rassoul's ear: "Who did you kill?"

"A woman."

Another family case, and thus of no interest. The judge has a watermelon pip stuck between his teeth, and is trying to dislodge it with the tip of his tongue. No luck. He continues, in a detached voice: "And the motive?" Silence, again. Again, the guard passes the question to Rassoul, who shrugs his shoulders to indi-cate that he doesn't know. "Was she his wife?"

"Was she your wife?"

"No," replies Rassoul at last, weary of these indirect questions and contemptuous stares. The judge pauses, not to think but to focus on the watermelon pip, the blasted pip. A new approach, with the index finger this time. Impossible. He gives up. "Who was it, then?"

"A woman called Nana Alia, from Dehafghanan," replies Rassoul before the guard can repeat the question.

"To steal from her?" asks the judge.

"No."

"Rape her?"

"No."

Again the interrogation pauses while the Qhazi has another go at the pip. He sticks his thumb and index finger into his mouth. There's no way he's going to do it. Rassoul would like to help him; his index finger is slim and bony, with a hard, tough nail. He has it down to a fine art: you have to push the pip with the end of your nail and suck it at the same time.

"Where are the witnesses?"

"There are no witnesses."

More and more enraged by the damned watermelon pip, the judge nervously tears the corner of a piece of paper from one of his files. He folds it and slips it between his teeth. Hopeless. As soon as it's wet the paper becomes floppy. The judge loses his temper, throws the paper down on the desk and asks, "Doesn't anyone have a match?" Rassoul immediately hands over his box. The judge takes one, removes the sulphur, sharpens it with his nails, and gets down to picking out the blasted pip. Success at last. Relieved, he stares at this aggravating speck, and then instructs the guards: "Let him go! I don't have the time to deal with this sort of thing."

"Come on!" One of the guards grabs Rassoul by the arm. But he remains standing in front of the Qhazi's desk. He will not move, he won't! He will rush at the judge, grab him by the beard, and shout: "Look at yourself, in me! I'm a murderer like you! So why don't you suffer?" He takes a step forward, but the guard's hold on him prevents further movement. "Qhazi sahib, you must judge me," he demands suddenly. The judge pensively strokes his own forehead for a moment and then says, spelling out the words to the rhythm of the prayer beads moving between his fingers: "Your case is a matter of *qisas*. Find the woman's family, and pay the price of the blood. That's all. Now, leave my office."

"That's all?"

Yes, Rassoul, that's all. You knew it would be, the clerk told you as much.

Y ES, YOU told me as much," admits Rassoul, sitting in front of the clerk's desk as he extracts the names of all the *shahids* executed in the communist prisons from a file. "But I thought I'd be able to persuade him to institute proceedings against me . . . and then against others, against all the war criminals." The clerk glances up at Rassoul ironically. "Where do you think you are?"

"Not anywhere, now."

"Welcome!" bids the clerk, returning to his task.

"And that exhausts me, too. This inability to make myself understood, or to understand the world."

"Do you even understand yourself?"

"No. I feel lost." A pause, long enough to travel far into a desert night. "I feel as if I have become lost in a desert night where there is only one landmark: a dead tree. Wherever I go, I see myself constantly returning to the same place, at the foot of this tree. I am weary of pathetically traveling down this same interminable path, over and over again."

"Young man, I once had a brother. He was an actor at the Kabul Nendaray theatre. He was always happy,

189

and liked the good things in life. He taught me an important lesson: to approach life as if it were a play. Treat every performance like it's the first time you are performing that role. This is the way to give all your actions new meaning."

"But I'm tired of playing the part I'm supposed to play. I want a new part."

"Changing the part won't change your life. You will still be on the same stage, in the same play, telling the same story. Imagine that this trial were a stage—which is exactly what it is, in fact; and what a stage! I could tell you some stories about that . . . Anyway, on this stage, at each performance you have to play a different part: first the accused; then the witness; then the judge . . . deep down, there is no difference. You know all the parts. You . . ."

"But when you play the judge's part, you can change the outcome of the trial."

"No, you are condemned to respect the rules of the game, to say the same things another judge has said before you . . ."

"In that case we need to change the play, the stage, the story . . ."

"You would be sacked!" The clerk raises his voice: "'Tis all a Chequer-board of Nights and Days / Where Destiny with Men for Pieces plays:/ Hither and thither moves, and mates, and slays, / And one by one back in the Closet lays.' That's not mine, it's Khayyam. Think on it!" Before Rassoul can get him back to the theater of the law, the clerk pushes the imposing file of *shahids* toward him. "It's your turn to help me out, now. Dictate those names to me!"

"I can't bear *shahids*!" This statement troubles the clerk. He looks at Rassoul for a long time, before reaching out to take back the file. Rassoul stops him: "But I will help you." He reads out the names. He has gone through barely a dozen when the Qhazi's guards reappear.

"Look, he's still here!" says one, pointing at Rassoul. "We were looking for you in the next world. You're coming with us!"

And they take Rassoul back to the Qhazi, who asks to be left alone with him. He is still behind his desk, prayer beads and handkerchief scattered among the papers. Apropos of nothing, he asks: "Do you know Amer Salam?"

"Amer Salam? I think so."

"Have you met him?"

"Yes."

"Where?"

"At Nana Alia's house, I think."

"When was that?" asks the judge, leaning across his desk in anticipation of a secret.

"The day after the murder."

"What the hell were you doing there?"

"My fiancée used to work for Nana Alia. Amer Salam came . . ."

"Where are the jewels you stole from her?"

191

At last, things are taking shape; at last they're interested.

Yes, that's true, but what the judge is most interested in is the jewels, not the murder, or your conscience, or your guilt, or your trial . . .

That doesn't matter, as long as I can use the jewels to force open the door of the law. Anyway, implicating Amer Salam in the case might be a way of tracking down the woman in the sky-blue chador.

"Have you gone deaf or what?" The judge's vehemence dislodges Rassoul from his train of thought.

"I told you. I didn't steal anything. I just killed her."

"You're lying! Amer Salam had pawned several pieces of jewelry with her. Give them back to him! Or he'll choke them out of you! You don't know what kind of man he is."

"I'm telling you that I didn't steal anything."

The Qhazi takes off his cap and uses his handkerchief to wipe away the beads of sweat gathering on his shaved head. "Come on, spit it out! I don't have time to waste on this case."

"But, Qhazi sahib, I swear to you that I wasn't able to steal them."

"So what happened to the jewels?"

"That is the great mystery . . ."

"Don't take me for an idiot! Give me back the jewels, and then go to your house and stay there!"

"You must listen to me. I didn't come to hand myself over to the law for nothing . . ."

"Well, why are you handing yourself over to the law?" asks the judge, finally realizing the absurdity of this enigmatic surrender. "Where the hell are you from?"

"It's a long story."

"I don't give a damn about your story. Tell me what faction you're from!"

"None."

"None!" The Qhazi is stunned. For such a man to take such a position in this war-torn land makes absolutely no sense, of course.

"Are you Muslim?"

"I was born Muslim."

"Who was your father?"

"He was a soldier. He was killed."

"He was a communist." That's it, here we go again. Always and forever the same questions, the same suspicions, the same judgments. I've had enough!

You wanted to tell him your story, didn't you—your life story? Well then, play the game. See it through.

"Your father was a communist, huh?" Is that a question, or a judgment? "Huh?"

"Sorry?"

"Your father, was he a communist?"

"Oh, that was a question."

The enraged judge loses his temper. "You too, you were a communist!"

"Qhazi sahib, I have come here to confess a murder: I murdered a woman. That is my only crime."

193

"No. There is something shady about all this. You must be guilty of more than that . . ."

"Qhazi sahib, is there a crime more serious than the killing of another human being?"

The question causes the handkerchief to fall from the judge's hand. "I'm the one who asks the questions! What were you doing in the communist era?"

"I worked at the Pohantoun library."

"So, you must have done your military service under the Russian flag." The judge picks up his prayer beads. "Tell me, how many Muslims did you kill?" It's a good job he doesn't know that you were in the USSR, or that would be the end of everything.

"I didn't do my military service."

"Then you must have been in the communist youth league."

"No, never!"

"You weren't a communist, you didn't do your military service, and you're still alive." Rassoul is silent. The only sound is that of the prayer beads slipping between the Qhazi's fingers. Suddenly he becomes angry again. "You're lying! You ungodly communist!" The beads stop moving, and in a black rage the judge calls for the guards. "Get this pig out of here! Shut him in solitary confinement! Tomorrow, blacken his face before punishing him in public: cut off his right hand for the theft, and then hang him! Whip his filthy corpse as a lesson to others: this is the punishment for survivors of the former regime who spread evil and corruption!"

The two armed men throw themselves on Rassoul
and grab him. He is dumbfounded.

He does not breathe.

His heart heaves.

The room crumbles.

The prayer beads once again begin slipping through the
Qhazi's fingers, one at a time.

Cries of fury invade the room.

Clanking chains excruciate the ear.

WHERE DOES the clanking come from? From your feet, your hands.

He moves. His feet and hands are heavy.

Heavy too are his opening eyelids.

Everything is dark. He is lying on a mat in a tiny room. Gradually, he becomes aware of the sky, far away, purple, framed by a small window covered in wire mesh at the very top of the wall. He sits up. The clanking of the chains echoes through the room, out the door, and into the deserted corridor. Rassoul moves toward the door and tries to open it with his bound hands. No handle. He pushes but it doesn't open. He bangs. He shouts. No response. Just these chains clanking in the silence of the night. He stops, defeated. Is it already over?

Here?

He bends down. Touches and explores the chain around his ankles.

I had barely recovered my voice.

Already, I am doomed.

Already, I am dying.

Dying, without a word, the final word?

He huddles his head between his knees.

He does not weep.

Suddenly, there is the abrupt sound of a door opening, and then footsteps shuffle down the corridor. He springs up, bends his ear to the door. The footfall approaches and then stops. The jangling of a bunch of keys, and the door opens. The harsh light of a torch scours the gloom, blinding Rassoul. A young bearded man points his gun at Rassoul and then waves in someone who has remained in the corridor. The face of the clerk appears. He comes in carrying a small tray in one hand, and a weak lantern in the other. Rassoul rushes forward to greet him. "Don't move!" screams the guard. The clerk turns toward him: "In the name of Allah, don't shout so loud!" and comes into the cell to hand Rassoul the tray. "We told you to stay and eat with us, and you didn't want to. You seemed in a hurry to get here . . . so, are you happy now?"

"No."

"But this is what you wanted, isn't it?"

"Yes, but not like this."

"How, then? Did you think they would take you to the Intercontinental Hotel, in a flower-strewn car, with an orchestra playing?"

"I'm talking about the sentence, not the welcome. This sentence without a trial. I don't want to leave the world without saying anything, without having the last word."

"Who do you think you are? The Prophet? Because your name means the Holy Messenger?" The clerk puts the lamp on the ground. "Sit down and eat something!"

"Where is Commandant Parwaiz?"

"Who is Commandant Parwaiz?"

"The head of security for Kabul; he works at the Ministry of Information and Culture."

"So?"

"I want to see him."

"It's already dark. They've announced a curfew tonight. There's a lot of fighting outside; even a fly wouldn't risk the journey. I'm going to stay here with you for a while." He says to the guard: "We would like a few minutes together. Can you take off his chains? I swear he won't try to escape. Don't worry. He came here because he wanted to."

"And he'll leave because he wants to, as well!"

"I'll take responsibility. You know me. He's a Muslim too. He's made a mistake—let him unburden his heart."

The guard thinks for a moment and then yields, asking for a little tobacco. Rassoul offers him his pack. "He smokes Marlboro, the bastard!" He takes two, returns the pack, and leaves.

The clerk sits down. "Come on, eat something." He pushes the tray toward Rassoul, who isn't hungry, or doesn't feel like eating.

"Eat! You'll feel hungry once you start eating. Give

yourself a little nourishment so that your blood can irrigate your brain; that way you might understand something! Why must you joke around with these guys?"

"I'm not joking. I want to be sentenced because I'm a murderer, not because my father was a communist."

"You are either naïve, have never lived in this country, or don't know anything about Islam and *fiqh*. You know, in sharia, killing someone is a crime dealt with by *qisas*: an eye for an eye, a tooth for a tooth. And that's it. It is a sentence concerned with the claims of man, so the victim's family decides the punishment. You, on the other hand, as a communist, represent *fitna*, discord. Therefore, you are judged by the law of *hudud*, equal penalty, a punishment established by the claims of God. Do you understand? I hope this isn't a riddle for you."

"I understand perfectly. But first of all, my father was a communist, not me! And . . ."

"No, you don't understand anything! Since when has anyone been judged as an individual in this country? Never! You are not what you are, but what your parents and tribe are. But perhaps that's a little complex for you. Come on, eat something!"

"Even you don't take me seriously."

"I take you seriously, but I don't understand you, because even you don't really understand what's eating at you. Is it guilt? Or the absurdity of your crime?"

"Neither. It's a profound discontentment with life."

"Now don't mix things up. It's because you are struggling to come to terms with your crime, your guilt . . ."

"I'm struggling to come to terms with my crime, because it hasn't surprised anyone. And no one understands it. I am weary. Weary and lost . . ."

Weary and lost, and with these five words suspended in his soul: *What is to be done.*

It is dark, and the clerk cannot see these words in Rassoul's eyes the way he saw them in the eyes of the donkey.

He must tell this old man the Nayestan story. Perhaps he will understand it.

So he tells him.

This time, he lingers on two moments in the tale. First, the strange feelings he had in the reeds at the end of the day, when he woke from a deep sleep: "I was invaded by a feeling of dread—vague at first, and then palpable. It was accompanied, bizarrely, by a strange sense of detachment. A detachment that didn't come from inside me; it was there, in the sky, the reeds, the wind, outside me . . . Everything was slipping away from my body, my spirit, in a word from my *djan.* Everything was moving away from me. Where did this sense come from? The empty sky? The breeze in the reeds? My father's futile waiting? I still don't understand."

After that, of course, he describes very closely the look in the donkey's eyes. This time, he reads another feeling into that look: "It wasn't only expressing his helplessness, *What is to be done,* but also his weariness, begging: 'Do away with me!' That's what the donkey was asking. It didn't understand what had happened.

It felt condemned to walk up and down the same path forever. Therefore, it wanted to die. And because it was unable, it was asking us to carry it out. By forcing its execution on us, it also made us reflect on our own situation, our own lot."

The clerk gives Rassoul a piece of bread, and takes one for himself. As he dips his bread into the stew, he says, "That is a beautiful story. It reminds me of one by Mullah Nasrudin. One day, Mullah returns home happy and full of joy. His wife asks him why. Mullah replies: 'I've lost my donkey.' His wife retorts: 'And that makes you happy?' He says: 'It does! I'm happy because I wasn't riding the donkey when I lost it, or I would have lost myself, as well!' I know this isn't the time to be telling funny stories, but your story made me think of it. You were lost because the donkey was lost. And today, you want to be condemned to death because that is what the donkey taught you! It is good, very good, to learn everything from everything: even the desire to die, and especially from a beast." He stands up. "Tomorrow, as soon as dawn breaks, at first prayers, I will search out your commandant. Now eat, and sleep." He takes his lantern and leaves, reciting in the silence of the corridor: "*The Revelations of Devout and Learn'd / Who rose before us, and as Prophets burn'd, / Are all but Stories, which, awoke from Sleep, / They told their fellows, and to Sleep return'd.*" He disappears into the black intensity of the night.

*　　*　　*

201

Rassoul sits down. His cell has been invaded by the smell of food. Repellent. He picks up the tray and carries it out. At the end of the corridor, a weak light ruptures the darkness, drawing Rassoul to a half-open door. He finds the young guard smoking a joint. Rassoul hands over the tray and the guard thanks him, and offers him a drag. "I've been here eight months. You are my first and only prisoner. Didn't you have anything better to do than hand yourself in, and create work for us? What did you do?" he asks, stuffing some bread into his mouth.

"I killed someone."

"Your father?"

"No."

"Your mother?"

"No."

"Your brother?"

"No."

"Your sister?"

"No. No one in my family. I just killed an old woman."

"In vengeance?"

"I don't know."

They fall silent, sleepy, staring blankly at the wreaths of smoke flowing up from the burnt wings of an owlet moth, come to honor the lantern's flame.

A RAY of light shines through the window, illumin-
ating a section of damp, crumbling wall covered
in prisoners' graffiti. A philosopher has scribbled
"Everything passes in the end"; someone who must have
been in love: "Love is not a sin," and finally, a poet:

I myself am stupefied
And by dreams occupied,
The world entire is deep in slumber,
I, impotent to speak; they, incompetent to hear.

Rassoul knows the graffitti off by heart. He has
already heard it, already read it. But it is the poem that
intrigues him most. Who wrote it originally, and then
on this wall? When? And for whom?

For me.

He walks up to the wall and runs his hand over the
writing. But the sound of footsteps striding up the
corridor freezes his fingers on the letters. Someone opens
the door and several armed men burst into his cell, their
faces hidden in the gloom. Rassoul huddles into himself,
before glancing up at the sound of a familiar voice.

"And how is our *watandar*?" It is Parwaiz, accompanied by the clerk and two other men. Rassoul leaps to his feet: "Salam!" Parwaiz is surprised: "Well, now! You've got your voice back?"

"Yes, two days ago."

"Then you can tell me the whole story, at last. I want to hear it all, in your own words."

"I went to hand myself over to the law."

"So the court clerk told me," says Parwaiz. Rassoul continues: "The night I was first brought to your office, I had just committed a murder."

The commandant leaves the cell, motioning Rassoul to follow him. "There is no such thing as coincidence! Why did you kill?"

"Why? I don't know."

Parwaiz stops and stares at him: "Like all of us!"

"That may be. But . . ." He stops. The clerk takes his chance to interrupt: "Commandant sahib, he killed to save his fiancée."

"What did your fiancée do?" Parwaiz asks Rassoul, who finds himself unable to speak. He is ashamed, and his silence speaks louder than words.

"Nana Alia wanted to train her up . . ."

"Yes."

"You did right, then," says Parwaiz with a conviction that stuns Rassoul and provokes a laugh from the clerk behind him. Rassoul stops walking; he thinks I did right? Parwaiz is not taking me seriously, either—and he is Head of Security, a mujahideen, a man of the law.

He says: "What do you mean, I did right? It was murder, premeditated murder . . ." Faced with the commandant's silence, he falls silent again.

They enter the building that houses the Law Archives. The clerk leaves them at the door to a large furnished room, nodding at Rassoul as if to say not goodbye but *You idiot!*

Parwaiz drops into a battered old sofa and invites Rassoul to sit down opposite him. He continues, as if he had never stopped speaking: "In your position I would have done exactly the same thing."

"But what was the point—I wasn't able to change anything, for my fiancée or myself. It did no one any good. It has caused more suffering than good."

"To do good, one must first suffer . . ."

"Worse still, my life has become hellish. I've lost both my fiancée and the money . . . A murder for nothing . . . Even the body has disappeared. Everyone just thinks Nana Alia went to the countryside. Tell me, could any crime be more absurd?"

"First, tell me why you didn't see your crime through to its proper conclusion?"

"That's exactly what I've been asking myself. Perhaps because I wasn't able to . . ."

"Or because you didn't want to. Because you are not a thief. You are a good man."

"But it was also Dostoevsky's fault."

"Dostoevsky? What has your beloved author done now?"

205

"He stopped me from carrying the act to its conclusion."

"How so?"

"The moment I lifted the ax to bring it down on the old woman's head the thought of *Crime and Punishment* flashed into my mind. I was struck to the very core . . . Dostoevsky, yes, it's him! He stopped me from following in Raskolnikov's footsteps, becoming prey to my remorse, sinking into the abyss of guilt, and ending up in prison . . ."

"But where are you now?"

Rassoul lowers his head and mutters: "I don't know . . . nowhere."

"Rassoul-*djan,* you read too much. That's fine. But there's one thing you should know: your fate is written in one book and one book only: the *Lawh Mahfuz,* the 'Preserved Tablet,' written by . . ." he points up at the ceiling, where a few flies are buzzing around. "Other books cannot change anything, in the world or in a person's life. Listen: Was Dostoevsky able to change anything in his country? Was he able to influence Stalin, for instance?"

"No. But if he hadn't written that book he might have murdered someone himself. And he gave me this conscience, this ability to judge myself, and to judge Stalin. That in itself is huge, don't you think?"

"Yes, it is huge," agrees Parwaiz, before retreating into a long silence. Then he says: "That is why I congratulate you on your conscience and your act!" He smiles. "You managed to wipe out a loathsome element of our society. The death of this woman must have been a great relief to many people. In fact, that explains the disappearance of her body—it was probably her own family. And if you hadn't murdered her, someone else would have; Allah would have; a rocket would've fallen on her . . . who knows! So you must see that you have helped several people . . ."

"And what about me?"

"What about you?"

"What good has it done me?"

"You must see that you have done something important: you have restored justice."

"Justice! But what justice? Who I am to decide if someone lives or dies? To kill is a crime, the most horrible crime a human being can commit."

"*Watandar,* murder is a crime when the victim is innocent. This woman needed to be punished. She had done wrong to your family, your *namouss.* She had dishonored you. What you did is called vengeance. No one has the right to judge you as a murderer. The end."

"Commandant, my problem is not with how others judge me; my problem is with myself. This suffering which gnaws away at me from the inside, like a wound, a festering wound that will not heal."

"In that case, there are only two solutions: either you amputate the injured limb, or you grow accustomed to the pain." He takes off his *pakol,* turns his head, and points to the back of his skull. "Look at that."

Rassoul bends forward to look.

"Touch it."

Rassoul brings his hand up, nervously; his fingers brush the commandant's skull. "Can you feel anything?" Rassoul hesitates to reply, then suddenly pulls away his hand.

"Do you know what that is?" Parwaiz replaces his *pakol*. "A piece of shrapnel. It's been in my skull for years. It was during the jihad. I had come home to see my wife and son. The Russians had heard we'd come to the village, and they bombed it. Our house was hit by a rocket. A large fragment martyred my family, and a small fragment lodged itself in my skull. I never wanted to have it taken out. I wanted to live with it, so the pain would constantly remind me of my family's death. Throughout the jihad this piece of shrapnel gave me strength, and hope. A French doctor told me that unless I had it removed, I wouldn't live for more than ten years. But I don't want to live for more than ten years." A loud laugh to lighten his bitter words. "You too have a piece of shrapnel—an internal one, an internal wound, a wound that has given you strength."

"What kind of strength?"

"The strength to live, and to create justice."

A young man brings them breakfast. The commandant asks him for news of Jano. "No news. We still haven't found him."

"What do you mean? He hasn't just disappeared into thin air! Search everywhere!"

"I bumped into him four or five days ago," interrupts Rassoul.

"Where?"

"He invited me to drink tea with him in the Sufi *chai-khana*. Inside, he met some mujahideen with whom you carried out a joint operation during the jihad, against a Russian military base."

"Can you remember their names?"

"They had served under Commandant . . . Nawroz, I think it was." Parwaiz is looking more and more distressed. He tells the young man to go to the *chai-khana* and see what he can discover. After a moment's thought, he continues: "Take the case of Jano. He is my adopted son. The Russians destroyed his village and massacred his family. But he has a lion's will to survive, which stems precisely from his desire for vengeance." He falls quiet, to give Rassoul a chance to ponder his words.

"Your wounds are wounds inflicted by others. But I inflicted my own wound. Instead of increasing my strength, it is smothering me, leading me nowhere. Sometimes, I think I wanted to murder that old woman just to find out if I was capable of killing, like everyone else . . ." He lowers his head. Parwaiz pours more tea and Rassoul continues, as if talking to himself: "I saw that I wasn't cut out for it. The other day I wanted to kill someone else, and I didn't . . ."

"Perhaps that person was innocent?"

"Innocent? I don't know. But he had insulted my

fiancée, chased her out of the Shah-e do Shamshira Wali mosque."

"Is that all?" He puts the tea in front of Rassoul. "You can't kill without a reason."

"Perhaps I wanted to kill him in order to deal with my botched murder."

"But that murder would have been botched, too, because you had done it for no reason."

"I think that's what happens. You return to a job in the hope of forgetting the previous one that you think you botched . . . And that is how crimes continue, in a vicious circle. That's why I handed myself over to the law, so they could try me and put an end to all this."

"*Watandar*, you know that a trial only makes sense if there is a legal system to ensure that rights are respected. And what has become of the law and the government these days?"

"Are you, too, looking for vengeance?"

"Perhaps."

"Gandhi used to say, 'An eye for an eye leaves the whole world blind.'"

"He was right. But vengeance is deeply rooted in us, whatever we do. Everything is vengeance, even a trial."

"So the war will never end."

"Yes, it will. It will end when one camp decides to accept the sacrifice, and stop demanding vengeance. Which is why it is so important to yield, to come to terms with one's acts, crimes, and vengeances . . . until one reconciles oneself with the sacrifice. But who can do that? Nobody. Not even me."

Parwaiz understands everything. He is capable of anything. Don't let him out of your sight. It is your job to shake him up, to return him to his mission. All he needs is a sacrifice, an accomplice. You will be that sacrifice.

"I want a legal trial. I want to be sacrificed."

Silence, again. It is the look on Parwaiz's face that condemns Rassoul to silence. An admiring, questioning look. Rassoul continues: "This trial will bring an end to my suffering. It will give me the opportunity to expose my soul to all those who, like me, have committed murders . . ."

"Stop thinking you are that Dostoevsky character, please. His act only made sense within the context of his society, his religion."

"But what woke up the West was a sense of responsibility, deriving from a sense of guilt."

"*Mash'Allah!*" Parwaiz waves his hand around, knocking over his tea. "Bless the Lord for giving them that sense of guilt, or else what would the world be!" He bursts into sarcastic laughter. "You really do want to sacrifice yourself to your fantasies."

"I'd prefer to sacrifice myself to my fantasies than to sacrifice others. I want my death to . . ."

He is interrupted by a burst of gunfire, not far from the Wellayat. Parwaiz pours more tea as he waits for Rassoul to continue.

"I want my death to be a sacrifice . . ."

"This country doesn't need any more deaths, any more *shahids* . . ."

"But I've no interest in being a *shahid*!"

Stop right there, Rassoul! You've already taken this too far.

I still have things to say to him.

Things you have said a thousand times before!

Yes, but not to him. He will be able to understand me. He knows that the existence of Allah has no need for witnesses, or martyrs.

If he knows that, there's no point telling him. Finish your sermon: "I want my trial and my sentence to bear witness to these times of injustice, lying, and hypocrisy . . ."

"In that case, *watandar*, the whole nation must be tried."

"Why not? My trial will be on behalf of all war criminals: communists, warlords, mercenaries . . ."

There is a long silence. Parwaiz has stopped drinking his tea. He is elsewhere, his gaze lost in space. A long way away, beyond even the sun that beckons at the window. Suddenly, he stands up. "Go back to your life, *watandar*, and your family. Get out of here! In Afghanistan this filthy war, like all wars, has its own laws and its own rules." Rassoul stands up too: "But you are in a position to change those rules."

Parwaiz stares at him for a long while, then holds out his hand. "When that happens I'll let you know. *Ba amané Khoda*. Now go home!"

H E DOESN'T dare enter his room, on account of the little shouts and laughs emanating from it. He doesn't dare smash the joy filling his home. Silently, he inches open the door. Yarmohamad's daughters and two other children are playing, piling up his books to build houses. Their innocent hands waltz dolls from one story to another: "*Khala, Khala,* give me a light!"

"I don't have one, go upstairs!"

"*Khala, Khala,* give me a light!"

"I don't have one, go upstairs!"

"*Khala, Khala . . .*"

Rassoul remains on the threshold, warmed by the children's gaiety, unwilling to destroy this world where no one has a light. He leaves them to act out their dreams.

He goes back down the stairs. No sign of Yarmohamad, or Rona. He finds himself back in the street, where there isn't a soul in sight. The insolent sun penetrates his skin, boils his blood, gives rise to strange emotions, strange feelings of inner desolation.

All bodies are a burdensome ruin.

All bodies need ether.

Need hemp, now and forever.

There is no one in the *saqi-khana* except Mustapha, curled up in a corner next to an unlit chillum. Rassoul greets him: "Salam!" Mustapha sits up drowsily, nods his head in response, and asks, as if in homage to his friend Jalal: "Has the war begun?" "No," says Rassoul. Mustapha invites him to sit down. "Do you have a *tali* of hashish?"

"I wouldn't have come if I did."

Mustapha struggles to his feet and staggers over to the far end of the den, saying, "When Kaka Sarwar died, everyone left . . ."

"He died?"

"Yes, they killed him. One day, when he was really flying, he went to the mosque, strode up to the pulpit, seized the loudspeaker, and recited verse 18 from the Koran. You know, the one he was always quoting, the story of Gog and Magog." Mustapha prizes a loose brick from the wall and continues. "We were here. We could hear him. We heard the shots they fired at him." He rummages around in the hole and then with a stifled groan pulls out a scorpion by the tail. He drops it into the chillum. "This is all we have left to smoke," he sniggers sadly. He strikes a match and sets fire to the creature. Eyes closed, he inhales the smoke and holds it in his lungs for a long time. Then he passes the chillum to Rassoul, and curls back up in his corner. Rassoul takes a brief, hesitant drag, then another longer one. It burns as if he had swallowed both the scorpion and its venom. His throat seizes up. His veins pulse like small, injured serpents trying to surge out of his skin. He drops the chillum, leans against the wall, and pushes himself to his feet. The room is spinning. Everything goes black. The door is only two steps away, but it takes forever to reach.

Outside, the sky continues to beat down on his nerves, hard and sharp. Rassoul starts walking, more and more wasted on the scorpion smoke.

He needs shade.

He needs softness.

He needs Sophia.

You only ever think of her when you're high.

No, in my poetic abyss.

Or in your monstrous agonies. That's when you love her.

He arrives at her house. He wants to knock, but his hand just hangs in mid-air, like his thoughts.

What do you want from her?

Nothing.

Go back.

I just want to talk to her.

What more do you have to say? What have you said so far? Nothing. With or without your voice you have nothing to say, nothing to do, except brood on your distorted ideas.

215

No, I'm not going to go on about them now, I promise. I'll take her to the vineyards at Baghebala hill, like I used to, so our love can look out over Kabul. I'll tell her how beautiful she is. She will blush. I will fall at her feet and finally tell her that I prostrate myself before not only her innocent beauty, but also her suffering. And she will tell me that it is a long time since I've spoken to her so tenderly. I will tell her that I've had a great deal to say to her, but that the war hasn't given us time. And I will kiss her. She will reach out and grab my hand. I will ask her to come away with me. Far, far away. To a beautiful valley where no one has yet acquired the power of speech, or else they have never experienced evil. A valley called the *Valley of Infans Regained*.

The sound of footsteps in Sophia's courtyard drives Rassoul from the gate. Two women emerge, cloaked in their chadors; they pay him no mind and disappear down another lane. Who were they?

Sophia and her mother?

They didn't see me. Or else didn't recognize me. I don't exist. I am nothing anymore.

"Sophia!" His cry does not emerge, lost in his vocal cords like before. He leans on the wall and lets himself crumple to the ground. He hugs his knees and rests his head on them. Shuts his eyes. Remains like that for a few moments, an eternity.

Here, he will stay.

Here, he will die.

Here.

And it has been years and years, an eternity even, that he has been here, at the foot of the wall.

It has been years and years, an eternity even, that he has been waiting for Sophia.

And Sophia never sees him, never recognizes him . . .

"Rassoul?" Dawoud's voice makes him lift his head. The boy is standing right in front of him, a can of petrol in his hand. "Hello, Rassoul."

"Hey! You're not on the roof?"

"You think my mother would let me work in peace? Sophia is away a lot these days."

"Is she working?"

"Yes. At Nana Alia's still—the old woman has disappeared, and Nazigol is afraid to be alone. Sophia spends most of her time there, even nights. But she comes back to see us every now and then." He puts down the can of petrol. "It's heavy . . . And you, you don't come and see us anymore?"

"I'm here, you can see that."

The boy rubs his hands together and then picks up the can. "I have to go, my mother is waiting." He waits for Rassoul to stand up. "Are you coming?"

"I wanted to see Sophia."

"She's at home."

"No, I think she went out."

"Maybe. Come in and drink some tea."

"Another time."

* * *

217

Dawoud has barely gone into the house when Rassoul, after another moment's hesitation, knocks at the gate. Dawoud opens. "Don't tell either Sophia or your mother that I came." The boy nods, looking down, as if to let his sadness spill out over his feet and across the ground. He shuts the gate, taking Rassoul's despair with him.

Rassoul starts walking, but after three paces he stops, pulling the money out of his pocket.

I don't need this.

He retraces his steps and knocks at the gate a second time. Again, it is Dawoud who opens. Rassoul gives him the whole bundle. "Don't say anything about this, either. Give it to Sophia. Tell her you made it selling pigeons!" Staggered to again hold such wealth in his hands, the boy remains frozen at the threshold until Rassoul disappears in the dust whirled up by a passing truck.

At home, Rassoul does not see either Yarmohamad or his wife.

As he had hoped.

He goes up to his room. The children have left. Only the flies remain, buzzing around the tray of cheese and raisins. The napkin covering the food is completely black, black with putrefaction. As always, his bed is unmade, indifferent. The indifference has spread to the books scattered all around, their covers stained; to the dirty clothes heaped in a corner; to the empty jug lying on the floor . . .

Why is everything indifferent to my return?

He picks up a glass.

Everything is ignoring me.

He throws the glass onto his mattress, and stares out the window at the courtyard. It is empty, empty of the cries of children.

Nothing recognizes me now.

An undeterred mouse crosses the room.

How can I live with this indifference on the part of my belongings?

Kicking away his pillow, he stands for a long time in the middle of his room.

Nothing is worse than no longer belonging to your own world.

No object wants to possess me.

No person wants to judge me.

This acquittal may clear everyone else's conscience, but it deprives me of my crime, my act, my existence.

And it will remain this way for as long as the mystery of my act is unsolved. I need to find Nana Alia's body.

M Y DEAR Rassoul, killing to exist is the principle behind all killings," says the clerk, tucking his files under his arm. He hurries to the door out of the Archives office. Rassoul follows. "I'm not looking for philosophy now. I just want you to help me solve this mystery."

The clerk stops suddenly. "Do you take me for some sort of detective? You're not in a cop film, or an Agatha Christie novel! Go and see your protector, Commandant Parwaiz."

"I have. But all he can think about is the disappearance of his adopted son. People are saying he's been murdered, beheaded . . ."

"The *dance of the dead*!"

They fall silent. As they leave the building, Rassoul stops the clerk. "You are the only person who can help me. You know so much. You must have dealt with so many cases, heard so many stories . . ."

"Yes, I have! But never one like this! In your case, there is nothing I can do."

"But there is: you can help me find Nana Alia's body."

"Why are you so interested in her damned corpse?"

"Because it will prove that I killed."

"There's no need to prove that. Everyone knows you killed. If you're so keen to trail a corpse around the streets, you'd better get moving! Just this morning three beheaded and decaying bodies were found hidden in a tomb at the Dehafghanan cemetery. Go and tell them you're the murderer!"

Rassoul says nothing.

When they reach the Wellayat courtyard, one of Qhazi sahib's guards is waiting. He sees Rassoul and calls out: "What are you doing here?"

"Commandant Parwaiz spoke to Qhazi sahib yesterday; it's OK, everything is settled," replies the clerk, before saying to Rassoul, "We'll discuss your request another time. Now get out of here!"

"Yes, but . . . I don't know where to go."

"Go home, young man!"

The guard interrupts: "No, wait! He is a prisoner here."

"Not anymore."

"What do you mean, not anymore? The judge is looking for him. How could he have been released without the judge's permission?" He prods Rassoul with his gun. "Come on now, move!"

Stunned, the clerk walks up to Rassoul and mutters quietly: "You must be completely nuts! Your head smells of qhorma! The world would be better off if you'd stayed mute."

"I did go home, but everything refused to recognize

me, it was all slipping away from me, my books, my bed, my clothes . . . It was all rejecting me. I went to my fiancée's house. She no longer recognizes me, either . . ."

"Don't worry! Everyone here recognizes you," says the guard, who is now holding Rassoul firmly by the arm. He drags him over to Qhazi sahib's office. Their hasty arrival startles a pigeon that had been pecking about on the judge's desk. It flies around the room in a panic, bashing against the windows and then flapping toward the door. "Shut the door, quick!" the Qhazi shouts. Pointing at the pigeon: "The exhibit must not be allowed to escape!" The guard rushes to shut the door. At last the judge notices Rassoul and in a fury asks the guard and the clerk: "Where had he gone?"

"He had left his cell, Qhazi sahib!" says the guard. This makes the Qhazi even more enraged. "What do you mean, left his cell? Who gave him permission?" The clerk mumbles: "Commandant Parwaiz summoned him, he . . ."

"Who is the Qhazi here? Him or me? Get this man out of here! Take him back to his cell! Chain him up!"

The two men sitting in front of the judge's desk turn toward Rassoul. One is the caretaker of the Shah-e do Shamshira Wali mausoleum; the other is the old man who was feeding wheat to the pigeons. Both are startled to see Rassoul. The old man rushes over: "No, Qhazi sahib, no, this young man is my witness. He was at the mausoleum, he saw me . . ." The judge, surprised, gestures to the guard to keep hold of Rassoul; then, pointing to the old man now standing next to Rassoul, says to the clerk: "First, create a file for this man."

"What is the crime?"

"Theft of pigeons from the mausoleum," replies the judge, and the caretaker concurs: "He came to feed them every day, with wheat," he turns toward the judge, "with wheat, that is!" then toward the clerk, "giving wheat is a sin. After that, he stole the pigeons. Do you know why?" He turns toward the judge again, "to grill them and eat them. His neighbors told me. They told me they could smell meat cooking at his place every day . . ."

"I have never eaten grilled pigeons. *Lahawlobellah!* The Shah-e do Shamshira Wali mausoleum pigeons? *Lahawlobellah!* He is lying!" cries the old man, rushing up to the caretaker. "Do you know that slander is one of the greatest sins?"

"So what was that pigeon doing in your pocket?" asks the caretaker, before saying to the Qhazi: "I found it in his pocket myself." The pigeon flies around the room. The old man walks up to the judge, in great distress: "It was pecking in my pocket. The mausoleum pigeons trust me, they like me. Look!" He whistles, and the pigeon flies over to him and lands on his shoulder. "He trusts me." He implores the caretaker: "Do not lie, my brother! You, the guardian of the Shah-e do Shamshira Wali mausoleum, are you not ashamed, before Qhazi sahib and before God, of wrongly accusing a Muslim brother?" To Rassoul, he begs: "You saw me, the other day. Tell them what I was doing there . . ."

"This young man is mixed up in the story as well?" asks the Qhazi. Rassoul takes a step forward to say: "I only saw him once, two or three days ago. My fiancée and I had gone there to pray. And I . . ."

"Qhazi sahib, you are right," interrupts the caretaker. "They are in it together. This man arrived to steal the alms money. He had a gun, and wanted to kill me as well . . ."

"Why are you lying?" cries Rassoul, taking another step forward. The guard grabs him. "Yes, I went there to kill him, but not to steal. Just to avenge myself, but in the end I couldn't . . ."

"You get everywhere! Who are you, what are you?" demands the Qhazi, leaning over his desk.

"Qhazi sahib, allow me to tell you," interrupts the caretaker again, standing up. "He's a . . . forgive me, Qhazi sahib—may Allah fill my mouth with dust!—this man is a pimp. Yes, he came to the mausoleum yesterday, with a . . . forgive me, Qhazi sahib—may Allah fill my mouth with dust!—with a whore. I chased her out; and he, he wanted to steal the mausoleum's money. They didn't come to pray, they came to steal!" The pigeon flies in front of him. The judge shouts at Rassoul: "With an impure woman? *Fitna!* You know it was because of an impure woman that the holy man Shah-e do Shamshira Wali, whose sacred tomb lies in that mausoleum, lost his life." He turns toward the others: "They say that even after he was beheaded by the enemy, the holy man continued to fight valiantly, a sword in each hand. When he reached Kabul, an impure woman cast him the evil eye and he collapsed and gave up his soul. In the Hadiths, it is said: 'Never let an impure woman enter a sacred place.' And this man, he took an impure woman to this sacred place! Where the other one was stealing pigeons! What kind of Muslims are you?" He shouts at the clerk: "Write! Write that the punishment reserved for thieves shall be meted out to him," he points at the old man, "who is accused of the theft of pigeons from within the sacred mausoleum. May both his hands be cut off." The old man opens his mouth, horrified, unable to speak. The pigeon leaves his shoulder, flutters around the room and lands on the Qhazi's desk. The clerk walks up to the judge and whispers in his ear: "Qhazi sahib, may I venture to remind you that according to sharia law, the amputation of an individual who has stolen something that has no owner, from a public place, is not considered a valid punishment."

"For what reason?"

"Qhazi sahib, we asked Imam Ali if the penalty of amputation was applicable to the theft of animals belonging to nobody, from a public place, and the holy man replied in the negative."

"Are you trying to give me a lesson in sharia?"

"*Astaghfirullah*! It was just a reminder, most venerable Qhazi sahib."

"In that case I too will remind you of something: I am the Qhazi here. And I decree that this man's hands be cut off." The clerk passes a sheet of paper and a pen to the judge. "In that case I ask you, Qhazi sahib, to be so good as to write this down in your own hand."

"You too are disobeying me? And, what is more, treating me without respect?"

"Far be it from me to have the slightest disrespectful thought, most venerable Qhazi sahib. I merely fear that, the day when you are no longer here—may Allah keep you safe and sound in this world—I could possibly be accused of having written a decree that goes against sharia."

"Goes against sharia? My decree goes against sharia? Get out! Gather your things and get the hell out of here, as quick as a bullet!"

The clerk wishes to speak, but the judge signals the guard to throw him out. The old man takes the opportunity to sink to his knees and beg the Qhazi, who immediately interrupts him: "Shut up, shut up! It is not recommended to make judgments in anger." Then, to one of the guards: "Put him back in prison, and bring him here tomorrow!"

The guard takes the old man out, and the caretaker follows. Rassoul remains where he is.

"Have you brought the jewels?" asks the judge. Rassoul approaches slowly and says, "No."

"What do you mean, no! Why did you leave prison, then?"

"Because they told me that there was nothing here for me anymore."

"Who?" yells the judge, before calling the guard and ordering him to return Rassoul to prison. "Solitary confinement! And tomorrow, send him for amputation, and then hanging!"

B EHIND THE bars, daybreak appears, silent and uncertain. As the muezzins call the faithful to prayer, as the guns of vengeance awake, as Sophia lies in bed embracing her innocence, as Razmodin saves the family honor at Mazar-e Sharif . . . Rassoul forgets the world that has abandoned him. He is sitting in a corner of his cell. Waiting for no one. Nothing. He decides he will be mute again, and also deaf.

Yes. I no longer hear. I no longer speak.

We are not capable of speech,
If we could only listen!
Everything must be said!
Everything must be heard!
And yet
Our ears are sealed
Our lips are sealed
Our hearts are sealed.

He must write this poem down here, in this cell, on this wall. He searches the floor for a pebble or a scrap of wood. There is nothing. He'll have to use his nails, then. He starts scratching the words onto the flaking paint. It is hard. It hurts. He presses down. He bleeds. He keeps writing. He writes until footsteps approach and then stop outside his cell, until keys jangle in the corridor, until the door opens, and a harsh voice shouts: "Out!" At that point he stops writing and stands still, impassive, his eyes glued to the words.

Two armed men enter his cell, grab him by the arms and lift him up. They drag him silently to the courtroom. A great hubbub can be heard from behind the door: "Murderer," "communist," "money," "vengeance" . . . The same words he has heard a thousand times; words that used to frighten or amuse him, but today simply make him deaf. He no longer hears them.

The door is opened.

Rassoul walks in.

The room falls quiet.

Everyone is there, sitting on wooden chairs, filling up the room. All bearded, all wearing black or white turbans or *charmah*, *qaraqol* and *pakol* caps. All looking at Rassoul. He is calm. His gaze sweeps the room and comes to rest on Farzan, serving tea with his usual sad smile. Parwaiz is there, too, sitting alone in a corner, his expression gloomy, anxious, and upset, his eyes glued to the ground. Amer Salam sits next to the Qhazi, his chest puffed out. His fleshy hands rest on a stick as he recites his prayer beads. He stares down at Rassoul and waggles his head—impossible to tell whether he is saying "Here we are at last!" or praying.

The Qhazi gulps his tea; the other men copy him, noisily. Farzan leaves the room with a final, even more tragic glance at Rassoul. The Qhazi puts down his glass and signals to a new clerk sitting beside him that the trial may begin. The clerk stands up, closes his eyes, and recites a sura from the Koran. Once the sura is finished, the Qhazi asks Rassoul to move up to the bar.

"Introduce yourself!" Rassoul glances anxiously at Parwaiz and remains silent. The judge grows impatient: "I'm telling you to introduce yourself!" Silence. Parwaiz stands up.

"The boy is sick . . . he has lost his voice."

The Qhazi grows annoyed: "What do you mean, lost his voice? He was fine yesterday. And today he cannot speak!" Addressing the courtroom, "Muslim brothers, thanks to our jihad we overcame communism." Everyone immediately intones "Allah-o Akbar" three times. The Qhazi continues, "But survivors from that regime, ungodly people, are still active among our Muslim population today, committing crimes and disseminating evil. The individual you see before you is one such. Just a few days ago he savagely murdered a defenseless widow in order to steal her money and her jewels. Fortunately, he was arrested by those in charge of security for our mujahideen government, under the orders of our brother Commandant Parwaiz, here today."

Parwaiz is surprised; he tries anxiously to meet

230

Rassoul's eye, but Rassoul keeps staring stubbornly at the ground. Just as Parwaiz moves forward to speak, the Qhazi signals the clerk to recite another sura from the Koran. Everyone falls silent. At the end of the recital, the Qhazi continues: "Did the accused understand the meaning of this thirty-third verse of the sura?" Rassoul stares at him without replying. "Instead of learning Russian you should have learnt the language of Allah, you irreligious man! God said: *Indeed, the penalty for those who wage war against Allah and His Messenger and spread corruption on earth is none but that they be killed or crucified or that their hands and feet be cut off from opposite sides or that they be exiled from the land.*"

The men shout themselves hoarse chanting "Allah-o Akbar!" three more times. The judge takes a gulp of tea. "Rassoul, son of . . . What was your father's name?" He waits in vain, then: "Never mind. Rassoul, son of—, of adult age and sound mind, admits to having murdered a widow on 16 *assad* 1372 of the solar Hejri, and stolen her money and her jewels. The court thus finds him guilty of theft and murder, and according to Islamic sharia accords him the supreme punishment, namely amputation followed by hanging . . ."

As the men once again shout three times, "Allah-o Akbar!" a single voice protests: "This is not right!" In response, other cries fill the room: "It is right!"; "It is sharia!"; "It is deserved, deserved!"; "Therefore it is right!" . . . The protester tries to make himself heard:

"Cutting off his hands is right, yes . . ." He recites a verse of the Koran, which quiets the room, and then continues: "Qhazi sahib, today, as you have said, thanks to Allah . . ."—the room intones: "Allah-o Akbar . . ."—the man continues . . . "our country is ruled according to sharia law, which is the very essence of our Islamic State. You would like us to follow that law? In that case, everything must be strictly based on *fiqh*. To start with, this man has lost his voice . . ."

"But this *fitna* does have a voice, he is just pretending," says the Qhazi, before saying to the guards: "Yesterday, this *fitna* was speaking. You were there."

"Yes, Qhazi sahib. We bear witness that this *fitna* was speaking perfectly."

The Qhazi turns toward the man and instructs him: "So beware of falling prey to his tricks. Continue!"

"OK, forget his muteness. As the victim is a woman murdered by a man, according to our sacred law the murderer must not be hanged, as the price of the blood of a woman is half that of a man." Another man stands up to protest: "That is impossible."

"It is possible to execute the murderer if the victim's family pay the other half of the price to the family of the accused."

"Or else the murderer is absolved, if he gives a girl to the victim's family . . ."

More people start shouting: "Where are the victim's relations?"

"She must be avenged!"

232

"If she is not avenged, the spilled blood will weigh upon us."

"An eye for an eye!"

"One moment, please!" demands the Qhazi, reciting his prayer beads as he speaks: "There are other, more serious accusations against this man. A few days ago a Muslim, caretaker of the Shah-e do Shamshira Wali mausoleum, revealed in front of the accused and witnesses that this *fitna* took a prostitute to the sacred site. What is more, he threatened the caretaker with a gun, in order to steal the alms money. The murderer admitted in front of witnesses that he wished to kill this caretaker."

"The man deserves to be hanged," cries one of the men. "He threatened an innocent?!" exclaims another. "That is a sin!" confirms the room. "Kill the caretaker of Shah-e do Shamshira Wali? *Lahawlobellah!*"

"That is a crime!"

"An affront to Allah and the saints!"

Amid all the racket, Rassoul feels nothing. He is impervious. He merely glances briefly at Parwaiz, who is watching the courtroom in silence. The shouts of the judge finally succeed in quieting the room. "There was a reason, at the beginning of this trial, that I told you the murderer was a survivor of the previous regime. This man confessed to me, of his own accord, that he has turned his back on the Holy Religion."

The shouts become frenetic: "The Devil!"

"Ungodly man!"

"Renegade!"

"He deserves to be hanged!"

The piercing voice of the judge again quiets the room: "Yes, brothers, you see before you a man who, according to the Koran, is *fitna*, the incarnation of Evil on Earth. This requires the punishment reserved by sharia for thieves guilty of murder and for renegades. Therefore, on Friday morning, after the call to prayers, in public at Zarnegar Park, this man will have his right hand and left foot amputated, with the limbs stuck on pikes for everyone to see. Then, this *fitna* will be hanged and displayed for three days as a lesson to the people. The prostitute who accompanied him to tarnish the tomb of Shah-e do Shamshira Wali will be stoned. In this way we will eradicate evil from our peaceful city . . ."

"Allah-o Akbar!" three times.

So this is your trial, Rassoul. Satisfied?

I haven't heard a word. What are they saying?

Nothing.

Sad and bitter, Parwaiz approaches Rassoul and addresses the courtroom. "Brother Muslims, I do admit that Qhazi sahib's words are most pertinent and convincing. But I will allow myself a few comments. Neither I nor the forces of order arrested this man. He came of his own accord to hand himself in."

"Why did he come of his own accord? There must be a reason!" exclaims the Qhazi, arrogantly thrusting out his chest.

"Yes, Qhazi sahib, there is a reason. I will explain it to you," continues Parwaiz. "I have met this young man several times. The first was when my men brought him to my office. His landlord had denounced him for non-payment of rent. That evening, he really had lost his voice. It was clear to see. And the last time I saw him was when he had regained his voice, and came to confess that he had killed a woman. He killed a madam to save his fiancée from her filthy clutches. Given the person in question it seemed to me necessary to carry out an investigation; an investigation that revealed no body, no witnesses, and no proof of this murder. No trace of it at all."

"Like all murderers, this vicious man has destroyed all the proof," says the Qhazi. Parwaiz walks back toward Rassoul. "If that were what he meant to do, he would never have come here of his own accord, Qhazi sahib! Given all the murders committed in our city these days, even a child could have wiped out the traces of his crime. Have we been able to arrest the killer of our young girls? Have we been able to track down the murderer who has been pitilessly poisoning our wives and children?" He falls silent to give people time to think, and to become aware of the ghastliness in which they live. Are they capable of understanding what Parwaiz is saying?

"Now, let us suppose that there was a victim. It is not for me to tell you that, according to our *fiqh*, homicide occurs when the victim is *ma'sum ad-dam*, innocent and protected. In this instance, that was not the case. The victim was a madam, and therefore liable to punishment by stoning." No protest. "The conduct of this young man, who handed himself over to the law in order to be sentenced within the context of a public trial, seems to me exemplary. It is a dazzling lesson. If we all decided, today, on the example of this young man, to put our own activities on trial, we could conquer the fratricidal chaos that is currently reigning in our country."

"What exactly are you trying to say?"

"Are you comparing this *fitna* to the mujahideen?"

"You too, Parwaiz?"

"Who are you? A mujahideen, a liberator, a leader of your people, or a lawyer for this turncoat murderer?"

"Go to hell, Satan!"

"A curse upon you, Parwaiz!"

Parwaiz stands in the middle of the room. "There was no murder. Listen to me: this is an imaginary murder, the illusion of a murder, simply to put our own behavior into question!"

"He's a madman?"

"No, my dear brothers—not only is he not insane, he is absolutely lucid, and quite aware of his illusions. It is we who are mad, we who have no awareness of the crimes we commit!" Everyone stands up, yelling. "Listen to me! This young man is asking to be tried for an illusion . . ." The louder Parwaiz shouts, the more excited the men become. In the end they rush at him and surround him. It is chaos.

236

Rassoul is laughing.

Do not laugh. They will put you in the Aliabad asylum, with the madmen.

And where am I now?

I N HIS cell, the darkness is profound.
   A fly lands on his hand. He blows on it; it stirs
and flies away.

Filth!

Why such hatred and fury for this tiny creature?

Because it just bursts into this world.

It does not burst into anything. It lives in its world,
because it belongs to its world. It is you who come
from elsewhere. You who are bursting into a world that
is no longer your own. Look at this fly; see how lightly
it lives in its world.

Because it is not conscious.

It isn't conscious because it doesn't need to be. It just
lives its lightness, its death . . . as simple as that.

And then it lands on his hand again. He tries to shake
it off but his arm won't move. Is it the chain that stops
him lifting his hand, or the fly? The fly, for sure. It is
paralyzing him. Taking over his world.

He stretches his neck toward the fly so he can blow
it away again. Impossible. His body is as stiff and as
heavy as stone. They look at each other. It seems to

him that the fly wants to tell him something, in its incomprehensible language. Rhythmic words, almost a song: *Tat, tat, tat . . . tvam, tvam . . . asi . . .* Then it moves, flying off and landing on the wall. And suddenly Rassoul can lift his hand; it has become light. The chains have come undone without a sound. He stands up to catch the fly. On the wall he can see only its image, like a fresco. He touches it. The wall seems liquid, permeable. His hand passes into it. He doesn't resist. The wall swallows his hand. Now his whole body moves into it. Once inside, Rassoul freezes. An image on the surface, just like the fly whose song slices through the silence of the wall. *Tat, tat, tat . . . tvam, tvam . . . asi . . .*

"Allah-o Akbar!" The call to prayer startles Rassoul, pulling him from the wall of his sleep. Here he is, on the ground, his hands and feet bound in chains.

The hoarse voice of the muezzin fades away and everything drowns in the silence. Except the song of the fly, which is still playing peacefully and religiously inside Rassoul's head, *Tat, tat, tat . . . tvam, tvam . . . asi . . .*

It no longer disturbs him.

Nothing disturbs him anymore, not even the sound of footsteps stomping up the passage and stopping outside his door; not even the door that will never again open for anyone except death.

They open the spy hole only. The guard says, "Stand up, you have a visitor." Rassoul doesn't move.

"Rassoul!" It is Razmodin. Rassoul stands up slowly and looks through the hole at his cousin's horrified eyes. He walks up to the door. "What have you done now?" Rassoul shrugs his shoulders, as if to say nothing serious. But Razmodin is waiting for a word, a voice. As usual, there is nothing. His cousin loses his temper. "Say something, damn it!" His words ring out in the corridor. "Hey, calm down!" exclaims the guard. "I was in Mazar," says Razmodin. "I brought Donia and your mother back here. We went straight to your house. You weren't there. I took them to a hotel. I've been combing the city for you. No one knew where you were, not Sophia, not Yarmohamad . . . Everyone is worrying. In the end, some of Parwaiz's guys told me where to find you . . ." He stops, hoping to hear Rassoul say something for once. In vain. He continues: "Why make up this crazy story? Have you lost your mind?" Rassoul is impassive. "Do something before it's too late, for the sake of your mother, your sister, for Sophia . . ." He moves away from the door to speak to the guard. "Let me into the cell, brother."

"No, you're not allowed."

"Please. There's something in it for you. Here!"

"No . . . but . . . well, just for a minute, then."

"I promise."

The door opens and Razmodin enters. "I can't tell my aunt anything. You know how she'll suffer if she hears about your arrest." He grabs Rassoul by the shoulders and shakes him. "How can I tell them? Do

240

you want your mother to have a heart attack? Do you want Donia and Sophia to lose their minds from grief? How can you be so selfish?" Everything is over, Razmodin, everything. Rassoul has no ego left, no pride. He is abandonment itself. "Tomorrow, you will be hanged!" The quicker the better, so Rassoul can move on to other things! "Why are you laughing at me?" He is not laughing at you, just laughing. He is laughing with the angels of death. "Why won't you take life seriously? You're behaving like someone from Aliabad!" More seriously, then? Tomorrow will be a great day for him; you'd better believe it. Everyone will be there, everyone. A beautiful death!

Yes, I want to live my death at last. Lightly.

Razmodin gets to his feet, discouraged by Rassoul's laughing eyes and cheerful silence. "I'm going to bring your mother and Donia. Perhaps they will change your mind."

Rassoul stands up in protest. He shakes his head, eyes pleading, as if to say: "No, Razmodin, leave them in peace!"

They stand staring at each other. "If they don't find out today, they will tomorrow."

When I'm dead, I won't care.

"But why? All this because you killed some stupid madam?" asks Razmodin, taking a step forward. "Look around you: people are murdering each other every day. Parwaiz's men were laughing as they told me your story."

241

So much the better if I'm making people laugh at last—and with my murder, too!

Razmodin drops to his knees. "So you still think that a trial can change this fucking country? You're dreaming, my cousin. Dreaming . . ." He swallows a sob, stands up, takes Rassoul by the shoulders and shakes him again. "Wake up, that's enough, wake up! Let go of these crazy dreams!" Rassoul shuts his eyes. His hand moves, hesitates, then clasps his cousin in an embrace.

I've woken, Razmodin.

They stand there hugging for a long time, until the guard arrives. "You must leave now, brother. It is time for his dinner."

Razmodin abandons Rassoul. They look deeply into each other's eyes one last time. "I won't abandon you," he says. "I'll go and see the judge, I'll see everyone. I won't let you destroy your life."

He leaves the cell, determined but anxious. The guard shuts the door, and then the spy hole.

A fly lounges on the wall.

*T*AT, TAT, *tat . . . tvam, tvam . . . asi . . .*

Where do these paltry words come from? He's probably heard them somewhere before. In an Indian film, perhaps. It doesn't matter. The noise is soothing, it makes the filthy fly seem more attractive.

Rassoul whistles the tune to block out the world.

And he hears nothing. Not the engine of a car as it stops next to his window. Not the men's footsteps entering the corridor and approaching his cell. Not the key in the lock, the door opening, or the gruff voice ordering: "Stand up!"

He remains sitting.

Light floods in, revealing the forbidding face of Amer Salam. He asks for the two of them to be left alone for a few minutes. As soon as the others leave, Amer Salam grabs Rassoul by the neck, insults him briefly, and asks him what he has done with the money and jewels that he stole.

Rassoul shrugs his shoulders to indicate that he doesn't know. Amer Salam insists, swears that he will cut them out of his mother's stomach if he has to, and presses his gun into Rassoul's belly. Rassoul gazes at him without fear and then points to his throat, groaning to indicate that he cannot speak. Out of his mind with rage, Amer Salam yells for a pen and paper. He will give Rassoul five minutes to write down the location of the jewels and the money. "And if you don't, I'll use that paper to set light to your girlfriend's pussy!" With that, he stalks out of the cell.

Rassoul is brought pen and paper. He writes: "Leave my family alone. I will give you everything at the foot of the gallows." He hands the piece of paper to the guard.

Five minutes later the guards return. They take Rassoul out, his hands and feet still bound in chains.

Before they get into the van, one of the guards asks Rassoul if he has performed his ablutions. He nods yes, smiling. The van drives out of the Wellayat gate, onto the road, and accelerates. Rassoul is hunched over when he hears his name being shouted from a distance. He looks up to see Razmodin running down the empty street, shouting and waving at the vehicle to stop. Rassoul gazes at him serenely.

The van drives along. Rassoul looks at the few pedestrians hurrying in the same direction, toward Zarnegar Park.

Lately, the sky has never been so blue, or so distant. And the sun has never been so clear, or so close.

The van stops in the park, and everyone gets out.

Rassoul is absorbed by the birdsong. He gazes at the branches of the trees, looking for the birds so he can hum along with them: *Tat, tat, tat . . . tvam, tvam . . . asi . . .*

"Rassoul!" A woman in a sky-blue chador rushes toward them, lifting the corner of her veil. It is Sophia, in tears, and the armed men push her away on the instructions of the new clerk. They prod Rassoul forward. He is apathetic, indifferent to everyone watching him, even to Farzan who nods a greeting with his usual sad smile.

"Don't take him there!" It is Razmodin again, shouting from the back of the procession, out of breath. "Yes, Commandant Sir!" sniggers one of the armed men as he stops him from coming any closer. Razmodin desperately repeats the same words, over and over: "Listen to me, this is awful, awful!"

The men push Rassoul forward; Sophia and Farzan follow behind. Suddenly they all stop, at the sight of the noose-less gallows surrounded by a silent crowd.

"Where is the noose?" demands the clerk. "It's been cut!" exclaims one of the guards.

They rush forward and join the crowd at the foot of the gallows. "Let us through, brothers, we have the convict. Move back, move back!"

People turn toward Rassoul and move back as he approaches. A corpse is revealed, lying on the floor. Everything freezes: time, breath, tears, words. Legs tremble. Rassoul falls to his knees beside Parwaiz's body, the noose around its neck. The crowd murmurs, fidgets, backs away. Other armed men appear and furiously push people aside to make way for the commandants, who arrive in a great cacophony. With their boots, everything disappears. Rassoul can no longer see. There is only the voice, nothing but the voice, Sophia's voice.

YOU'RE BEAUTIFUL," Rassoul whispers in Sophia's ear. She blushes. He throws himself at her feet to tell her at last: "I prostrate myself before not only your innocent beauty, but also your suffering." She is moved. She contains herself. Only her hand responds, slipping into Rassoul's hair to lose itself there. "It's been a long time since you've spoken to me so tenderly."

"I've had a great deal to say to you, but the war hasn't given us time."

He kisses her, shyly, on the cheeks. She hides her face, reaching out to take Rassoul's hand. "Will you come away with me?" he asks her.

"Where?"

"Far away."

"To Mazar-e Sharif?"

"No, further . . . to the *Valley of Infans Regained*!"

"Where is that?"

"It's a long way away. Not to the east or the west, not to the north or the south."

"It doesn't exist, then."

"I will build it for you."

"How will it be?"

"A beautiful valley, where no one speaks. Where no one has ever experienced evil."

"So we are the *infans*?"

"Still and always!" And they laugh.

"I have to go now," she says, standing up.

"Are you going back to Nazigol's place?"

"No. She left with Amer Salam."

"Where did they go?"

"I don't know." She moves closer: "I hope they don't come to the Valley of Infans Regained!"

"No. It is only for us."

"See you soon, then!" She puts on her sky-blue chador and leaves the cell.

Rassoul remains standing, lost in thought. "You have another visit," the guard tells him. And the old clerk comes in, carrying a thick file. "How is our young man?" Rassoul nods his head, feeling calm.

The clerk is about to sit down, but Rassoul won't let him. "Don't sit there, please. There is a fly, a poor fly . . ." The clerk is intrigued. He puts on his glasses and peers at the floor. Then he moves to one side, and sits down very carefully. "This fly . . . it is imprisoned with me," says Rassoul as he points to the creature, which has settled languidly next to the clerk.

"So now you're even worried about the life of a fly?"

"Last night, I had a strange dream. I dreamt of this fly humming a song that I knew, something like *tat, tat, tat . . . tvam, tvam . . . asi . . .*—yes, that was it, but I couldn't make out the meaning."

248

"It's an Indian song."

"That makes sense. What does it mean?"

"'You too are this'!"

"That's pretty."

"Now even the flies are singing for you. Life is beautiful! So are you happy that your trial is turning out as you wished?"

"It's all the same to me now."

"All the same to you? You've turned the world upside down and it's all the same to you? Because of you, an important mujahideen leader has hanged himself; the judge has been fired; the newspapers talk of nothing else day and night; your cousin has involved all the foreign journalists and UN officials . . . and what does Sir say?" The clerk shakes his head in disapproval.

"It wasn't me who turned everything upside down. It was Dostoevsky!"

"That's it, you're off again. Stop going on about your precious Dosto-whatever! You didn't kill because you'd read his book. You read it because you wanted to kill. That's all. If he were still alive, he would accuse you of plagiarism!"

Rassoul looks into the clerk's eyes for a long time. "Don't look at me like that. I didn't ask you a riddle," says the clerk as he spreads out his papers on the floor. "In any case, they gave me my job back, and they want a file on you . . . By the way, do you know what they found in Commandant Parwaiz's pocket?"

Rassoul's eyes are bright with curiosity. "They found

a letter, in his handwriting: '*Mourn me, don't avenge me!*' What a man, what a brave man! Do you know why he committed suicide? Apparently his troops found the man who had killed his adopted son. But in the confrontation, the murderer's wife and baby were also killed. Now, moving on . . . what should I write, please?"

Silence.

"Everything! I've told you everything . . ."

"Everything? I don't think so. In any case, I've already drafted a few lines. I'll read, and if there's a problem you can point it out: *The moment Rassoul lifts the ax to bring it down on the old woman's head, the thought of* Crime and Punishment *flashes into his mind. It strikes him to the very core. His arms shake; his legs tremble. And the ax slips from his hands. It splits open the old woman's head, and sinks into her skull. She collapses without a sound on the red and black rug. Her apple-blossom-patterned headscarf floats in the air, before landing on her large, flabby body. She convulses. Another breath; perhaps two. Her staring eyes fix on Rassoul standing in the middle of the room, not breathing, whiter than a corpse. His* patou *falls from his bony shoulders. His terrified gaze is lost in the pool of blood, blood that streams from the old woman's skull, merges with the red of the rug obscuring its black pattern, then trickles toward the woman's fleshy hand, which still grips a wad of notes. The money will be bloodstained* . . . So, tell me, why didn't you take the money?"

Acknowledgments

My utmost gratitude to all those who have blessed this novel:

Laurent Maréchaux and Denis Podalydès for their valued reading;

Danièle D'Antoni and Leili Anvar for their germane comments;

Rahnaward Zariab, Kambouzia Partovi, Hafiz Assefi, Rahima Katil and Sajad Zafar for their "Persian perspective" and support;

Paul Otchakovsky-Laurens for everything;

and Christiane Thiollier and Sabrina Nouri forever.

Atiq Rahimi was born in Afghanistan in 1962 and fled to France in 1984, where he has become an award-winning author (2008 Prix Goncourt) and filmmaker (2004 Prix un certain regard, Cannes). The film adaptation of his novel *The Patience Stone*, which he cowrote and directed, was selected as the Afghan entry for the 2012 Oscar for Best Foreign Language Film. In recent years, he has returned to Afghanistan many times to set up a writers' house in Kabul and offer support and training to young writers and filmmakers. He lives in Paris.

Polly McLean is a freelance translator from Oxford, England. Winner of the 2009 Scott Moncrieff Prize, she has translated books by Catherine Deneuve and Sylvia Kristel, as well as the award-winning *Secret* by Philippe Grimbert.